100 GREATEST LEADERS

Ana Clifton is an educator with an experience of around two decades. Passionate about holistic education, Ana has helped transform the lives of hundreds of students, many of whom are employed in prestigious roles across the world. Ana holds a Bachelors in Education and a Masters in Literature, and loves to experiment with learning delivery so that learning is fun and interesting. Apart from teaching, Ana directs plays, trains students on public speaking and debating. She specializes in honing the creative side of learners through participant learning. Her other interests include music, history, art and culture.

100 GREATEST LEADERS

Ana Clifton

RUPA

Published by
Rupa Publications India Pvt. Ltd 2019
161-B/4, Gulmohar House,
Yusuf Sarai Community Centre,
New Delhi 110049

Sales centres:
Bengaluru Chennai
Hyderabad Kolkata Mumbai

P-ISBN: 978-93-5333-549-6
E-ISBN: 978-93-5333-550-2

Seventh impression 2025

10 9 8 7

The moral right of the author has been asserted.

Printed in India

CONTENTS

INTRODUCTION

The task of the leader is to get their people
from where they are to where they have not been.
—HENRY KISSINGER

The world is witnessing tumultuous times. While the issues of poverty, malnutrition and conflict have become the mainstay in many parts of the world, migration, global warming and parochial nationalism are other broader issues that are troubling humankind. The need is to create a new breed of leaders and statesmen who can stand up and lead us through this quagmire.

Fortunately, the youth is not only aware, but wants to stand up to shoulder responsibility as agents of change. They must be empowered to usher in the next level of change that the nations today deserve.

The 100 leaders who have been discussed in this book are men and women who stood up for the transformation that they have brought about, or yearn to bring in their nations. Their accomplishments make them stand tall as statesmen and visionaries who try to transform entire generations. They have heralded such change that the ripple effects can be felt far and wide.

The seeds of becoming an agent of change are sown in our minds. One of the objectives of this book is to enable young minds to appreciate the efforts and the sacrifices that the leaders make, to bring about change. The challenge for our times is to not only accept change but also to honour it.

This book aims to make better denizens of the world who are eager to evolve into world citizens. These leaders are legendary and uncompromising. While Abraham Lincoln gave a new face to the United States, Mahatma Gandhi gave a new meaning to leadership. Martin Luther King Jr stood up for his race and Vladimir Lenin stood up for liberty and fraternity. The spiritual guidance of Swami Vivekananda is invaluable.

At the same time, these unforgettable men and women are people like you and me who have had their role models, their fears and have seen failure. And yet, they have emerged victorious; some are still creating history. This book will show you the grit and determination that kept them going despite everything.

This book, *100 Greatest Leaders*, is a product of consistent efforts and research for over a year. Hope the readers enjoy the book and gain insight into the lives of these people.

ABDULLAH II

Unconventional, daring and modern, King Abdullah II of Jordan never expected to be the king. Yet, he has been ruling Jordan with élan and has already made an indelible mark on the country.

EARLY LIFE

Abdullah was born on 30 January 1962 to King Hussein and his second wife, English-born princess Muna al-Hussein. His upbringing had both privileges and hardships. King Hussein wanted Abdullah to grow up with the knowledge of the ways of the world. Therefore, Abdullah was sent to a boarding school in the United States (US) from where he completed his primary as well as high school. Abdullah grew up acquainted with American customs and beliefs, and was grateful that his father gave him the opportunity to develop a global perspective and appreciate different cultures. However, young Abdullah always wanted to come back home.

After his graduation in 1980, Abdullah was sent to join the Sandhurst Military Academy in England to take formal training so he could become an able soldier in the Jordanian Army. He soon became the head of the Jordanian Special Forces. This made him very popular among his subjects.

CORONATION

King Hussein expired on 7 February 1999. Just two weeks before his death, he named Abdullah as his heir apparent. Although Abdullah's uncle was supposed to inherit the throne, Abdullah was coronated as the king. With such great responsibility entrusted upon him, Abdullah's life changed and he realized that his life was meant to be dedicated to the kingdom.

Though King Abdullah continued with his father's pro-western philosophy, he wanted to create a positive image of his kingdom.

Many reports suggest he went undercover to get a first-hand understanding of the issues his kingdom was facing.

MILITARY AND ECONOMIC DEVELOPMENT OF JORDAN

Jordan shares its borders with Syria, Iraq, Israel and parts of Saudi Arabia, which makes it distinct from other Middle Eastern countries. King Abdullah upgraded his armed forces to maintain the sovereignty of his kingdom even though peace with neighbours was his primary objective.

King Abdullah has brought many reforms in the kingdom including a free market and vocational training centres across the country to reduce unemployment. He has reformed the energy sector and also took the initiative to provide houses to his people, especially the teachers, and people from the armed forces.

MEETING ENERGY NEEDS

Earlier, Jordan was dependent on Egypt for oil as it was not a petroleum-producing country. However, to make his country self-reliant in the energy sector, King Abdullah decided to develop other reliable sources of power.

By 2025, Jordan is expected to have two 1,000 MWe nuclear plants. Several solar energy plants have come up, and many more are being commissioned. A liquefied natural gas port has also been set up for generating electricity.

POLITICAL REFORM

Abdullah has initiated many political reforms in the country. Emphasis has been laid on the judicial and human rights of the people. One of the most laudable steps taken by him was curtailing the power of the king. He has amended the constitution and established an independent Election Commission. Laws were formulated under him for the protection of women against violence and women-friendly trial procedures.

DID YOU KNOW?

- Abdullah loves adventures and thrills. He is a champion rally car driver, sky diver and scuba diver.
- Despite being the king, he leads a very normal life. He even helps his wife toss up a meal on weekends.
- Abdullah II is the 41st descendent of Prophet Muhammad.

ABRAHAM LINCOLN

Abraham Lincoln is an embodiment of the fundamental American ideology and a symbol of determination. In every respect, Abraham Lincoln, the 16th president of the US, is a legend.

EARLY LIFE

Abraham Lincoln was born on 12 February 1809 to a humble couple, Thomas and Nancy Hanks Lincoln, in a frontier log cabin in Kentucky. After his father lost most of his land there, the family decided to move to Indiana in 1816 to avoid hardships. In 1818, young Lincoln lost his mother.

Life was not easy in Indiana. Lincoln was raised to work in a farm and received no formal schooling. Lincoln stressed on the importance of reading and writing in shaping a person's life. He went to school for only a year or so. In 1831, Lincoln left home for New Salem where he tried various occupations including being a captain in the Black Hawk War that gave him a new purpose in life.

ENTRY INTO POLITICS

Lincoln strived to become a lawyer even though he had received no formal education. Interestingly, he learnt law by reading books. In 1836, he was admitted to the bar where he began practising law, and earned quite a reputation for his honesty and was popularly known as 'Honest Abe' in the legal circuit.

Meanwhile, Lincoln also tried his hands in politics and earned a seat in the House of Representatives. Lincoln belonged to the Whig Party and therefore, was primarily focused on the economic progress of the nation.

LINCOLN'S TAKE ON SLAVERY

Lincoln was losing interest in politics when the Congress passed a legislation allowing the spread of slavery. Lincoln termed it immoral, and in 1856, he joined the newly-formed Republican Party and campaigned against Stephen A. Douglas for the senate. In his speech, he made it clear that the nation had to be completely slave-free. Even though Lincoln did not win the seat, he achieved considerable national fame for his views.

LINCOLN'S RUN FOR PRESIDENCY
Lincoln won the nomination to presidency in 1860. As his ideas of eliminating slavery grew, his supporters increased. Interestingly, Lincoln did not give any presidential speech; instead, he monitored the activities of the party minutely and motivated its members. In November 1860, Lincoln was elected as the 16th president of the US. But even before Lincoln assumed office, seven states seceded to form a new constitution of their own, declared their sovereignty and called themselves the Confederate States of America. Suggestions to compromise flowed in but Lincoln stood his ground and said, 'I will suffer death before I consent...' Lincoln made several attempts to make the states join the union but, they all refused and war loomed large over the country.

THE CIVIL WAR AND ELIMINATION OF SLAVERY
The American Civil War began on 21 April 1861. It was started by the Confederates, a group of eleven states that wanted to protect the institution of slavery. Lincoln quickly formulated some strategies to combat the war. Eventually, the Civil War ended on 9 April 1865 with the surrender of General Robert E. Lee in Virginia. Lincoln, as the commander-in-chief, abolished slavery as a military necessity. While the preliminary Emancipation Proclamation came on 22 September 1862, it was followed by the final one on 1 January 1863 that abolished slavery completely.

Lincoln also amended the constitution, calling slavery unlawful. This was a momentous victory for the entire country. He made it compulsory to include the freed slaves into the army and also proposed ways to rehabilitate them. He wanted to build the US on the tenets of forgiveness and generosity.

ASSASSINATION

The nation mourned the assassination of Abraham Lincoln on Good Friday, 14 April 1865. He was assassinated by John Wilkes Booth, a Confederate sympathizer.

DID YOU KNOW?

- Lincoln had a pet cat whose name was Tabby. It used to have dinner with him at the White House dinner table.
- Lincoln is considered one of the most influential American presidents and is revered the world over for his honesty and integrity.
- Abraham Lincoln kept his important documents inside his hat.

ADOLFO SUÁREZ

Spain still stands in awe of Adolfo Suárez, the first democratically elected prime minister of the country. He was the architect of democracy in Spain and followed it by bringing in big reforms.

EARLY LIFE

Adolfo Suárez González was born on 25 September 1932 at Cebreros near Spain. His father was a civil servant while his mother was from a highly influential political family. Suárez earned a degree in law at the age of twenty-one and went on to obtain a doctorate degree from the University of Madrid.

Suárez worked in various positions during the regime of Francisco Franco, the dictator of Spain. The National Movement was the sole political party during that time and Suárez became the minister secretary general of the party. He has also been the director general of the Spanish Radio and Television Corporation before joining politics.

ENTERING POLITICS

Things took a different turn with the death of the dictator Francisco Franco in 1975. By then Suárez had joined the National Movement party, the sole party in power in Spain for thirty-eight years, and held the position of secretary general. Suárez voiced his opinions about allowing more political parties and making the selection of the leader more democratic.

On 3 July 1976, King Juan Carlos appointed Suárez as the prime minister of Spain and proclaimed that his government would be the product of the free will of the Spanish people. His decision met with a lot of opposition, but King Carlos supported his will to establish democracy in Spain. Suárez legalized socialist and communist parties in Spain which had been suppressed by the Franco government.

PRIME MINISTER OF SPAIN

Suárez founded the political party, the Union of the Democratic Centre, which consisted of liberals and democrats. When free and fair elections were held in 1977, Suárez's party became the undisputed winner, with Suárez as the first democratically elected leader. But peaceful establishment of democracy was not easy due to a strong opposition, and the terrorist group—Basque Euskadi Ta Askatasuna (ETA)—had again become active. Suárez resigned from politics in 1981.

CONTRIBUTION

Suárez tried to bring in some reforms by legalizing trade unions and weakening the military's influence over the government.

LATER LIFE

After retiring from politics, Suárez became a member of the Club de Madrid, which is an organization of former prime ministers and presidents formed to strengthen democracy and governance. Suárez passed away on 23 March 2014. He shall always be looked upon as a man who helped Spain transition to democracy without spilling a drop of blood.

DID YOU KNOW?

- Suárez was the man behind the first television channel in Spain.
- Suárez had correctly predicted a month before the death of Franco that democratization could not be stopped and that the National Movement party could not last for long.
- In recognition for his contribution to democracy, King Juan Carlos of Spain conferred upon him the title of Duke of Suárez and Grandee of Spain.

ANGELA MERKEL

A ngela Merkel has pushed boundaries and created new horizons for herself, her nation and the whole world. The first female chancellor of Germany, she is a key architect of the European Union and one of the towering female leaders of the world.

EARLY LIFE

Angela Dorothea Kasner was born in Hamburg, West Germany, on 17 July 1954, to a Lutheran pastor and a teacher. She was the eldest of three children. The family moved to Templin, and Merkel grew up in the countryside of East Berlin.

Merkel loved to learn different languages at school and was even awarded a prize for her proficiency in Russian. From 1973 to 1978, she studied physics at the University of Leipzig and later worked and studied at the Central Institute for Physical Chemistry of the Academy of Sciences in Berlin-Adlersh of from 1978 to 1990. After being awarded a doctorate for her thesis on quantum chemistry, she worked as a researcher and published several papers.

ENTRY INTO POLITICS

The fall of the Berlin Wall was a turning point in the history of Germany and it served as a catalyst to Merkel's career. Merkel was attracted to the new democratic movement and joined the new party—Democratic Awakening. In 1990, Democratic Awakening merged with East German Christian Democratic Union (CDU).

Merkel contested the first post-reunification parliamentary elections and was elected to the Bundestag from the Stralsund-Nordvorpommern-Rügen constituency. She was appointed as the minister for women and youth in the cabinet under Chancellor Helmut Kohl, who became her political mentor. Soon, she was promoted as the minister for environment and nuclear safety.

POLITICAL CAREER

After the Kohl government was defeated in the 1998 elections, Merkel was appointed as the secretary general of the CDU, which allowed her to take independent decisions. Merkel oversaw a string of CDU election victories and soon become the first female leader of the party on 10 April 2000.

Merkel could not win the election, but became the leader of the opposition in the Bundestag. She argued in support of reforms, and laid stress on the German-American relationship.

CHANCELLOR OF GERMANY

In the 2005 national elections, Merkel won the CDU/Christian Social Union (CSU) nomination as a challenger to Chancellor Gerhard Schröder of the Social Democratic Party of Germany (SPD). She enjoyed popularity among her countrymen and announced in her campaigns that her government would try to reduce unemployment and initiate economic reforms. In the elections, Merkel defeated the incumbent chancellor by a narrow margin. The CDU had to agree to form a coalition government with the Social Democrats, and Merkel was declared the chancellor of Germany, the first woman to assume that position.

True to her words, Merkel worked relentlessly to remove unemployment and establish better relations with other countries. Merkel was elected for the second time in 2009, winning by a good margin.

MILESTONES AS CHANCELLOR

Merkel has crossed many milestones as the chancellor. Her domestic policy is aimed at building a nation where people from different nations dissolve their boundaries and adapt to the German world. Her foreign policy too is founded on the desire to bridge the gap between Germany and other nations, and strengthening European cooperation and international trade.

Merkel's agenda of transatlantic economic relations saw her

reaching out to Asian countries and the US. Merkel won a third term as the chancellor in 2013 and led her party to victory for the fourth term in 2017.

DID YOU KNOW?

- Merkel was attacked by a dog in 1995, and since then she has had a fear of dogs. When Putin brought his pet Labrador for a press conference in 2007, Merkel got scared and observed, 'I understand why he has to do this–to prove he's a man... He's afraid of his own weakness.'
- Merkel has been awarded doctorates from several international universities.
- In May 2016, Forbes named Merkel as the 'Most Powerful Woman in the World' for a record tenth time.

A.P.J. ABDUL KALAM

Avul Pakir Jainulabdeen Abdul Kalam, popularly known as Dr A.P.J. Abdul Kalam, stands out as one of India's finest presidents. Fondly known as the 'Missile Man of India', he was an able administrator, professor, and a versatile individual, which made him one of India's most admired leaders.

CHILDHOOD AND EARLY LIFE

Kalam was born on 15 October 1931 to a Tamil Muslim family, boat owner father Jainulabdeen and mother Ashiamma, in Rameswaram, Tamil Nadu. Since his childhood, Kalam was a hard-working boy who spent hours studying, especially mathematics. After graduating in physics from Madras University in 1954, he studied aerospace engineering from Madras Institute of Technology.

KALAM AS A SCIENTIST

After becoming a member of the Defence Research & Development Service (DRDS), Kalam joined the Aeronautical Development Establishment (ADE) of Defence Research & Development Organization (DRDO) as a scientist. The first thing that he designed as a scientist was a hovercraft for the Indian Army. After a brief period of working under the famous scientist Vikram Sarabhai, he was transferred to the Indian Space Research Organisation (ISRO) where he was the project director of India's first Satellite Launch Vehicle (SLV-III), which successfully deployed the satellite Rohini in near-earth orbit. Dr Kalam also directed Project Valiant and Project Devil that aimed at developing ballistic missiles using the technology of the SLV programme, which was another great success.

These aerospace projects remained classified under the direction of Dr Kalam. He was made the chief executive of the Integrated Guided Missile Development programme which was meant to develop a quiver of missiles. Under his guidance, the team developed missiles like Agni and Prithvi.

Kalam was the secretary of the DRDO from July 1992 to December 1999. He was also the chief scientific advisor to the prime minister in 1992. Dr Kalam played a pivotal role in the 1998 Pokhran-II nuclear tests. In 1998, he, along with cardiologist Dr Soma Raju, developed a low-cost coronary stent, which was named 'Kalam-Raju Stent'. They also designed a tablet PC for healthcare in rural areas called 'Kalam-Raju Tablet'.

PRESIDENCY

Dr Kalam served as the 11th president of India from 25 July 2002 to 25 July 2007. He was affectionately known as the 'People's President'. During his tenure as the president, Kalam made it a priority to meet, one-on-one, as many young people as possible, setting a target of 5,00,000 for his five-year term. Even after leaving office in 2007, 'Kalam Chacha' (Uncle Kalam), as he was fondly called, would receive hundreds of emails a day from young people inspired by his exhortation to 'dream, dream, dream'!

ACCOLADES AND RECOGNITION

Kalam received seven honorary doctorates from forty universities. He was also decorated with the Padma Bhushan in 1981 and the Padma Vibhushan in 1990 for his work with ISRO and DRDO and his role as a scientific advisor to the government. In 1997, the Bharat Ratna, the highest civilian award, was also conferred upon him for his contribution to the field of scientific research, development and modernization of technology in defence. A prolific writer, his writings have been translated into many languages and have inspired many people.

SAD DEMISE

Dr Kalam lived the life of a 'Karma Yogi' and even died like one. He died of cardiac arrest while delivering a lecture on 'Creating a Liveable Planet Earth' at the Indian Institute of Management, Shillong, on 27 July 2015.

DID YOU KNOW?

- In an official visit to the Vikram Sarabhai Space Centre as the president, he took time off to visit George, a cobbler who used to repair his shoes.
- He used to sell newspapers as a young boy.
- As the president of India, he used to donate all his savings to an NGO named PURA (Providing Urban Amenities to Rural Areas).

ATAL BIHARI VAJPAYEE

An iconic leader, an able statesman and a man of unflinching determination, Atal Bihari Vajpayee, three times prime minister, stood tall as one of India's finest leaders.

EARLY LIFE

Atal Bihari Vajpayee was born on 25 December 1924 at Gwalior in Madhya Pradesh. His father, Krishna Bihari Vajpayee, was a poet and school teacher. Young Vajpayee was highly impressed by his father; he wanted to follow in his footsteps and become a poet as well. After his schooling from a government school, he graduated from Victoria College, Gwalior. He then moved to Kanpur for a master's degree in political science. Being a patriot to the core, Vajpayee joined the Rashtriya Swayamsevak Sangh (RSS) in 1939, with the sole objective of rendering his services to the cause of the nation.

FREEDOM FIGHTER

Vajpayee started his political career as a freedom fighter. He participated in the Quit India Movement in 1942 and was also imprisoned for the same. It was during this time that he met the legendary leader of Bharatiya Jana Sangh, Shyama Prasad Mukherjee, from whom he took his first lessons in politics. After the death of Mukherji, all the responsibilities of Bharatiya Jana Sangh came to rest upon Vajpayee's shoulders.

POLITICAL JOURNEY

Vajpayee played a significant role in Indian politics after independence. He was chosen as the member of parliament from Balrampur, Uttar Pradesh, in 1957. Vajpayee was made the national president of the Jana Sangh Party in 1968, after which his entire focus was on working for his party.

To be able to serve the country better, he formed the grand alliance by joining hands with the Janata Party. He participated with Jayaprakash Narayan in the 'Total Revolution', against misrule and corruption in the government of Bihar. It later turned against Prime Minister Indira Gandhi's government and the Emergency imposed by her. When Morarji Desai became the prime minister, Vajpayee joined his cabinet as the minister of external affairs. However, the alliance was short-lived.

FORMATION OF THE BJP

After the resignation of Morarji Desai, the party began to disintegrate. Atal Bihari Vajpayee, along with Lal Krishna Advani and Bhairon Singh Shekhawat, formed the Bharatiya Janata Party in 1980. Vajpayee became the first president of the party. The party became a strong critic of the Congress(I) government that took over after the fall of the Janata Party. Vajpayee also raised his voice against Operation Blue Star and the 1984 anti-Sikh riots after the assassination of Indira Gandhi.

PRIME MINISTER OF INDIA

The people of India found Vajpayee's wisdom appealing. They saw in him a leader who gave them hope for a better future. He was sworn in as the 10th prime minister in 1996. But the government lasted for only thirteen days, as Vajpayee could not obtain a majority. Vajpayee again came back to power and served as the Indian prime minister in 1998–99 and 1999–2004, during which India underwent a tremendous change. Vajpayee sent out a message across the world that India was ready to embrace growth and development.

Vajpayee was a great statesman. He conducted nuclear tests in Pokhran which was acknowledged by the world. In equal steed, Vajpayee also made honest efforts to improve India's relations with Pakistan by inaugurating the historic Delhi-Lahore bus service. But Pakistan betrayed the initiative and started the Kargil War where India gave a fitting reply.

Vajpayee heralded India towards economic reforms and encouraged the growth of private sector industries. Many road projects were undertaken under him across the country. His health started failing, following which he retired from active politics in 2005. He breathed his last on 16 August 2018.

DID YOU KNOW?

- Vajpayee is often compared to Bhishma of the Mahabharata for his wisdom and experience.
- He has been awarded with India's highest civilian awards–the Bharat Ratna and the Padma Vibhushan.
- Vajpayee and his father were classmates when they pursued the study of law at Kanpur.

AYATOLLAH ALI KHAMENEI

Ayatollah Ali Khamenei, one of Iran's greatest leaders, is a person who changed how the West viewed the Middle East. He challenged the US and stood against its brutal might with unflinching determination.

EARLY LIFE

Khamenei was born on 16 July 1939 in the holy city of Mashhad, a province of Khorasan. His father was a humble Islamic scholar who led a simple lifestyle. Khamenei's early education consisted of learning the alphabet and the holy Quran. Later, he pursued a study of theology.

Khamenei was an exceptionally intelligent child. He was only eighteen when he started his higher studies related to religion. He visited all the holy shrines of Iraq, then returned to Iran and continued with his studies in Qom. Khamenei returned to Mashhad when his father lost vision in one eye. He began teaching scholars about religion and the Quran.

ENTRY INTO POLITICS AND RISE AS A LEADER

Khamenei, a devout cleric, was proud of Iran and wanted to safeguard its religious and cultural identity. The Shah, who was the ruler of Iran, advocated the western way of life and wanted to do away with the influence of Islam as the guiding authority. He believed that Islam could be the only uniting factor of Iran. Khamenei was influenced by the teachings of Imam Khomeini, the then religious leader of Iran, who gave him the spark to fight the Shah's despotism. The year 1949 saw the Shah of Iran growing in stature and power. Khamenei was still a minor threat for various political parties. As Iran was passing through a tumultuous time with more protestors against the Shah's police state, Khamenei started gaining support, and his speeches began drawing people. The Shah came to power again in 1953 after being overtaken for a few years by his political rivals. When him used brutal force to crack down on protestors, Khamenei spearheaded a revolt against the Shah and condemned his policies by calling them anti-Islamic. Khamenei's arrest on 5 June 1963 brought people to the streets, and a national figure was born. Despite the arrest, he continued to speak against the Shah's regime. Khamenei was soon deported, but this served as a unifying factor for Iranians.

Khamenei took refuge in Iraq and continued his agitation for almost a decade and a half. The more the Shah leaned towards the US, the more Khamenei strengthened his revolution. Khamenei wanted Islamic faith to be the guiding principle of the government. The Shah declared Martial Law in Iran in 1978 and arrested the party heads and clerical leaders. By the end of 1978, the Shah was losing, and fled Iran in 1979. Khamenei then returned to become the undisputed leader of Iran.

BEGINNING OF A NEW ERA

Khamenei wanted to form a government where the clerics played the dominant role. As a mark of protest against the American influence, the people of the American embassy in Iran were held hostage for more than 400 days by a group of college students who supported the revolution in 1978.

Khamenei continues to enjoy more power than the Iranian president. Iran is now a country that is proud of its culture and religion and does not believe in aping the West.

DID YOU KNOW?

- As a young boy, Khamenei was interested in poetry and literature of Iran and wanted to pursue his studies in it.
- All the pictures of Khamenei where he was smiling were destroyed after the revolution with the intention of projecting him as a stern leader.

BARACK OBAMA

Barack Obama dared to dream, and channelled his passion to achieve the impossible. He was the 44th president of the US and its first black president.

EARLY LIFE
Barack Hussein Obama II was born on 4 August 1961 in Honolulu, Hawaii to Barack Obama Sr and Ann Dunham. When he was two years old, his parents separated. At the age of ten, Obama was sent to Hawaii to stay with his maternal grandparents.

Obama graduated in 1983 with a degree in political science and entered Harvard Law School in 1988. Having excelled at the law school, he found his calling—to make a difference to people and communities. Between 1992 and 2004, Obama practised civil rights as a lawyer and also taught constitutional law at the University of Chicago Law School.

LAW TO POLITICS
Obama joined politics after he won a seat in the state of Illinois in 1996. Obama worked with both democrats and republicans as a state senator to draft legislation on ethics as well as to expand healthcare services and early childhood education programmes for the poor. In 2003, Obama became chairman of the Illinois senate's Health and Human Services Committee.

CAREER IN US SENATE
Obama dreamt big and even his unsuccessful attempt to win a seat in the House of Representatives could not deter him from trying for the senate. Obama opposed George Bush and spoke against his war with Iraq. In November 2004, Obama was sworn in as a senator after receiving 69.9 per cent of the votes, which is the largest electoral

victory in the history of the state of Illinois.

PRESIDENTIAL ELECTION

Obama announced his candidacy for the 2008 democratic presidential nomination and centred his campaign on hope and change. He won the election with a thumping majority and was sworn in as the 44th president of the US.

Obama took over the office against the backdrop of a number of challenges such as economic recession and ongoing foreign wars. Obama hit the ground running and started working for bettering healthcare and economic growth. He overhauled the foreign policy and improved relations with other countries, withdrew all US troops from Iraq and initiated a reform to make healthcare affordable for Americans. For his persistent efforts, Obama was awarded the 2009 Nobel Peace Prize.

SECOND INNINGS

The campaign for the second presidential term also focused on the grassroots and a promise to take the US to newer heights. His major victory came when a bill regarding spending cuts and tax increase was passed. The bill agreed to raise the federal deficit by raising taxes for the extremely wealthy.

In 2013, when Syrian leader Bashar al-Assad had used chemical weapons against civilians, Obama pressurized al-Assad to give up chemical weapons. He also entered into a dialogue with Iran and thawed their relationship.

Obama was also very concerned about the degrading environment and proposed new regulations on power plants, factories and oil refineries. He also introduced some gun-control measures like background check of gun sellers.

MAJOR BREAKTHROUGH AND LEGACY

Obama's major breakthrough came when he was able to establish relationships with Israel, Libya, Cuba and Africa. His surgical raid on Osama Bin Laden was hailed by Americans and nations across the world.

Barack Obama's presidential term ended on 20 January 2017. He will always be remembered for being a humane president who was able to face challenges head-on.

DID YOU KNOW?

- Barack Obama won a Grammy in 2006 for the audio version of his memoir, *Dreams from My Father*.
- He is inspired by Martin Luther King Jr, Mahatma Gandhi, Pablo Picasso and John Coltrane.
- He is a big fan of basketball. In fact, Obama was called 'O'Bomber' for his basketball skills.

BENAZIR BHUTTO

Fearless, assertive, charismatic and ambitious—these are some qualities that describe Benazir Bhutto, the Iron Lady of Pakistan, who stands out as one of Pakistan's greatest political leaders.

EARLY LIFE

Benazir Bhutto was born on 21 June 1953 to Zulfikar Ali Bhutto and Begum Nusrat Ispahani in Karachi, Pakistan. Her father had served as the prime minister as well as the president of Pakistan. He was also the founder of Pakistan People's Party (PPP). After her schooling in Pakistan, Benazir pursued her higher education in the US. Later, Benazir went to Britain to study international law and diplomacy. When her father was imprisoned for forming PPP, he used to write letters to her, which kindled Benazir's interest in politics.

JOINING POLITICS

Benazir returned to Pakistan in 1977 and joined her father, but he was overthrown in a military conspiracy. He underwent a trial and was executed in April 1979. Benazir and her mother were imprisoned for a year. After being freed, Benazir took over the reins of the PPP. The family was allowed to travel abroad in 1984 because of medical aid, and Benazir became a leader of PPP during her years of exile abroad. She returned to Pakistan in 1986 and conducted a nationwide campaign for the return of democracy.

TURNING OVER A NEW LEAF

In the 1988 national elections, PPP emerged as the undisputed winner. Benazir became the fourth female prime minister in the world and the first woman prime minister of a Muslim country. Apart from working for removal of poverty, corruption and crime, Benazir travelled to various countries to improve Pakistan's international relations. She also wanted to improve India-Pakistan relations and had talks with Rajiv Gandhi. However, she made it quite clear that if India improved her nuclear weapons, then Pakistan would not tow behind.

Later, there were allegations of corruption against Benazir, and the people also started losing faith in her. Ghulam Ishaq Khan seized the opportunity and dismissed her government.

LEADER OF THE OPPOSITION

Since PPP could not perform well in the 1990 elections, Nawaz Sharif became the prime minister and Benazir Bhutto took over as the leader of the opposition, but was placed under house arrest.

SECOND TERM AS PRIME MINISTER

Benazir Bhutto became the prime minister of Pakistan for the second time in 1993. She was also a founding member of the Council of Women World Leaders in 1996. To emancipate women, Benazir appointed women as judges and also set up a women's division in the government. She also established women's banks and all-female police stations.

She took control of the ministry of finance and tried to privatize industries, but some of her initiatives were sabotaged by her own cabinet. In her second term too, she was removed from power in 1996 on charges of corruption, and sent to exile.

ASSASSINATION

Benazir returned to Pakistan after eight years of exile, but in a tragic turn of events, she was assassinated by a suicide bomber during her election campaign on 27 December 2007.

DID YOU KNOW?

- In her childhood, Benazir was called Pinkie by her family owing to her being an unusually pink baby.
- When Benazir returned to Pakistan after her exile in Britain, she was given such a warm welcome that an 8-mile journey from the airport to a rally site took 9. 5 hours!
- Coincidently, she was assassinated in Rawalpindi, the same place where her father was hanged.

BENJAMIN NETANYAHU

Benjamin Netanyahu's leadership has been so profound that it has helped Israel steer ahead on the road to development, even in areas that it had never done before.

EARLY LIFE
Born on 21 October 1949 in Tel Aviv, Israel, Benjamin Netanyahu's father was a historian and an activist. Netanyahu's early childhood was spent in Jerusalem before the family moved to the US.

JOINING THE ARMY
After his return to Israel, Netanyahu enlisted in the Israeli Army. Exhibiting great leadership skills right from the beginning, he was an exemplary soldier, and easily outshone others.

Netanyahu participated in many army operations. There came a phase in his life when he felt that he was not satisfied simply being in the army and wanted to do something more. He thought of pursuing his education and, therefore, went back to the US where he received degrees in architecture and business administration from the Massachusetts Institute of Technology.

ENTERING POLITICS
On his return to Israel in 1978, Netanyahu got involved in the political matters of the country. He was a scholar and could have settled for a plum post and a secure life. But, he remained concerned about the terrorism rampant across the country and started the Jonathan Netanyahu Anti-Terrorism Institute as a tribute to his brother who lay down his life during a military operation.

From 1984 to 1988, he served as an ambassador of Israel to the United Nations (UN). He used this platform to condemn the Nazi atrocities. He joined the Likud Party in 1988 and was elected as a member of the Knesset (parliament). In the government, Netanyahu served as the deputy minister for foreign affairs. In 1996, he came to be seen as an able leader and was elected as the prime minister. Ever since, he has been the prime minister of Israel four times, in 1996, 2009, 2013 and 2017.

CONTRIBUTION

During his first tenure as prime minister, governance in Israel was highly imbalanced and the country was reeling under debt. Therefore, he focused on making his country a robust economy. He brought in a number of reforms which led to strong economic growth.

Israel's growth in terms of technology has been phenomenal under his leadership. Netanyahu reduced the taxes and urged youngsters to have their own start-ups, and passed many regulations to help the private sector by cutting down taxes and removing other barriers. He also trimmed the public sector to make way for the private sector.

Israel has never been as strong diplomatically, militarily and economically as it is now, and it is all due to the remarkable leadership of its prime minister. Under Netanyahu's leadership, Israelis have enjoyed one of the safest and quietest periods with regard to terrorism. He has also been able to establish harmonious relations, not only with the Middle East but also with other eastern countries like India, Singapore, Australia and China.

DID YOU KNOW?

- Netanyahu is the first prime minister of Israel to be born in independent Israel.
- He has his own fast food chain by the name of Fat Netanyahu Burger in Jerusalem.
- When he went to the US, he barely knew a word of English. His classmate, Julia, taught him basic English.

BILL CLINTON

A true representative of the great American dream, Bill Clinton, the 42nd president of the US, was an extraordinary administrator. He left behind a rich legacy that others could cherish and follow.

EARLY LIFE

Bill Clinton was born on 19 August 1946 in Arkansas, a small town in the US. Clinton never knew his biological father, as the former had died in an accident two months before his birth. While Clinton was in high school, he got a chance to go to Washington DC as part of a special youth leadership conference where he shook hands with John F. Kennedy, and that was when he developed an interest in politics.

After graduation, Clinton won a scholarship to the University of Oxford, where he studied philosophy, politics and economics. Then, he earned a law degree from Yale Law School, following which he started his private practice and also taught students.

ENTERING POLITICS

Clinton had always wanted to join politics. After several attempts, he was elected as the governor of Arkansas in 1978. He made many reforms in the education, healthcare and welfare sectors and was even voted the most effective governor by his peers. He announced his decision to run for presidential elections in 1992.

RUN FOR PRESIDENCY

Bill Clinton stood against President George Bush, who was quite a popular president himself. During the campaign, Clinton went on a bus tour around the country. His campaign emphasized family and moral values and how every American has a right to fulfil his or her dream. People loved him because Clinton offered hope and promise for the future. Clinton's magnetic personality combined with a well-planned campaign resulted in his victory and he was sworn in as the president of the US in 1993.

CONTRIBUTION

The year 1993 saw the start of the first presidency of the Democrats in a dozen years. In his first address to the nation, Clinton announced his intention to increase taxes taxes to meet the deficit in the budget. But, at the same time, he also cut government expenses. He desired that the economy of the country should thrive again. Clinton devised a national health care plan that would cater to all the Americans of any income group, one of the most significant items on Clinton's legislative agenda. Clinton helped in establishing peace in the Middle East, especially between Israel and Palestine. Clinton also tried to resolve the differences in the Arab countries like Syria, Jordan and Lebanon.

SECOND INNINGS

When Bill Clinton was re-elected in the 1996 presidential elections, he got the chance to sign a major healthcare bill, the Medical Leave Act, and turned it into law.

Clinton also pursued peace in northern Ireland by following in the footsteps of President Jimmy Carter and used his office to do enormous good. He is still considered a key player on the global stage.

DID YOU KNOW?

- It was at Yale Law School that he met his life partner Hillary Clinton.
- The Clinton Foundation does extraordinary work around the world.
- He is a Grammy award winner for his narration of *My Life*, in the category of Best Spoken Word Album.

BILL GATES

Bill Gates is one of the richest men on earth. His meteorical rise to such heights is a saga of inspiration.

EARLY LIFE

Born on 28 October 1955 in Seattle, Washington, William Henry Gates was very good at academics and was always inquisitive to know about new inventions and discoveries. He was also a voracious reader. When his school introduced a computer class in high school, he started spending most of his time there. He made his first computer programme at the young age of fifteen, for which he was awarded $20,000. With this, he entered the world of technology, and since then there has been no looking back.

CAREER

At seventeen, Bill Gates conceived of the idea of opening a company with Paul Allen, his senior. Although his parents wanted him to complete his studies first, Bill could not develop any interest in any subject, even though he tried. Meanwhile, he started working on BASIC, a programme for microcomputers.

FOUNDING MICROSOFT

The year 1975 saw the inception of Microsoft by two nineteen-year-olds, Bill Gates and Paul Allen. The company started doing so well that Bill had to leave his studies before his final year. Due to his dedication and hard work, Microsoft became almost parallel to established hardware companies like Apple, Intel, IBM, etc. By 1978, the sales of his software went up to $1 million. From only thirteen employees, the office strength went up to 128 employees. In 1980, IBM approached Microsoft to make its software and thus began a strong collaboration. By 1983, Microsoft's turnover catapulted to

$16 million and it was making software for companies across the world. Unfortunately, Paul Allen left Microsoft in 1983 owing to health issues. Thereafter, the entire responsibility of the company came on Bill's shoulders.

MICROSOFT WINDOWS

Bill Gates took the company to newer heights. The launch of Microsoft Windows brought a revolution to the world of computer technology. It made the use of software easier. He became a billionaire at the age of thirty-one!

In 1987, Microsoft lost its biggest customer as IBM replaced the software MS-DOS with its own software OS/2. Bill started upgrading Microsoft Windows, came up with new programmes and brought down the prices of his products so that he did not have competitors. By the age of forty-two, he became the richest American and had a monopoly on software programmes.

PHILANTHROPIC BILL GATES

Bill Gates, along with his wife Melinda French, formed the Bill and Melinda Gates Foundation for carrying out various philanthropic services. Being the largest private foundation in the world, it has reached out to various countries worldwide to reduce extreme poverty, and to provide healthcare and education.

Bill Gates, the co-founder of Microsoft, now owns only 1.3 per cent of the company's shares. He stepped down as the chairman of Microsoft in February 2014 and now occupies the position of a technology advisor to current CEO, Satya Nadella.

Bill felt the urge to give back to the world the money he has amassed. Therefore, he donated half of his wealth to the cause of charity. Many other key people have followed his example and have donated their money as well.

DID YOU KNOW?

- Bill Gates regrets not knowing any foreign language.
- Despite his immense wealth, his three children will only inherit $10 billion each.
- India has awarded the highest civilian award, the Padma Bhushan, to both Bill and Melinda for their philanthropic activities in the country.

BOUTROS BOUTROS-GHALI

Boutros Boutros-Ghali, an able diplomat and statesman, is widely regarded as one of the finest leaders to have led the UN. As the secretary-general of the UN, he settled some of the most complex issues in the world and left behind a trail of affirmative governance.

EARLY LIFE

Born on 14 November 1922 in Cairo, Egypt, Boutros Boutros-Ghali was born into a wealthy family and picked up the traits of a diplomat from his father and grandfather. After receiving formal schooling, he earned a law degree from Cairo University and then went to France to study public law and economics. He also had a doctorate in international law from Paris University.

EARLY CAREER

On his return to Egypt, he taught international law and international relations at Cairo University from 1949 to 1979. He was a renowned scholar and was invited as a guest lecturer to many universities in the world.

ENTRY INTO POLITICS

Ghali's political career started taking shape during the tenure of President Anwar el-Sadat. He was made the president of the Centre of Political and Strategic Studies in 1975. Ghali became the minister of state for foreign affairs of Egypt in 1977. His performance in improving relations between Egypt and Israel led Hosni Mubarak, the then Egyptian president, to induct him as the deputy prime minister for International Affairs.

INDUCTION TO THE UN

Assuming the office of secretary general of the UN in 1992, he led the mission of establishing peace between Israel and Egypt which he had initiated as the minister of state earlier. It finally found fulfilment during his tenure as the secretary general.

Ghali was a part of many complicated peace-keeping operations in the world. He said that the cold war among the countries needed to be addressed to avoid major clashes. The most important goal that Ghali nurtured was increasing the role of the UN in maintaining international peace and security. He also improved coordination among UN workers across the world.

Ghali set the target that by the 50th anniversary of the UN, he would have increased its importance and significance regarding international issues.

FACING CRITICISM

Boutros Boutros-Ghali was often criticized for being too moderate. However, his critics were soon miffed by his extraordinary diplomatic skills. He believed that democracy, development, peace and globalization go hand in hand. In his tenure, Ghali overlooked deployment of more than 70,000 UN peacekeeping troops. On 16 February 2016, the world lost a great diplomat in Ghali as he breathed his last.

DID YOU KNOW?

- Ghali and his wife were multilingual. They argued in Arabic and spoke lovingly in French. While talking about business, they spoke English.
- Late President Anwar el-Sadat used to call him Peter when he was happy with his performance.
- In one of his interviews, he admitted that he had been quite a bully in school.

B.R. AMBEDKAR

The messiah of India's lowest strata, Dr B.R. Ambedkar, swam against the tide and fought for the deprived and the downtrodden.

EARLY LIFE

Bhimrao Ramji Ambedkar was born on 14 April 1891 to Bhimabai and Ramji. His father was a subedar in the Indian Army who encouraged his children to receive education. Ambedkar was born into a Dalit family and was, therefore, exposed to social discrimination right from his childhood.

Since he was considered an untouchable, normal education was also denied to him. Luckily, the government had started a school for children of those who worked in the Indian Army which Ambedkar eventually joined. Despite being good at studies, he, along with other untouchable children, sat in one corner of the class, away from the children of higher castes. The teacher hardly paid attention to these children. Ambedkar was pained by this discrimination. He went to the US for post-graduation and eventually, also did his doctorate from there.

RETURN TO INDIA

Ambedkar returned to India in 1916 after he stopped getting his scholarship. In India, he worked as a clerk and an accountant so that he could save some money and go back to London to complete his research. Finally, he joined the London School of Economics and completed his research on 'The Problem of the Rupee: Its origin and its solution', which was a dream come true for him. He earned two doctorate degrees, and by 1923, having earned the law degree as well, he was one the most educated Asians.

Ambedkar returned to India and dedicated his life to the service of the society. India was fighting for her independence and Ambedkar immersed himself into the movement. He also started voicing his opinions about the social recognition and freedom of the Dalits. Ambedkar believed that for real freedom, India should abolish social discrimination. He began voicing his ideas through books which brought a revolution in the thoughts of the people.

ENTERING POLITICS

Ambedkar entered politics to remove the plague of untouchability from society. To achieve this, he reached out to people from all strata and explained the drawbacks of this social evil. He also proposed a separate electoral system for untouchables and other marginalized communities. Ambedkar launched full-fledged movements for Dalit rights in 1927 and demanded that the public drinking water sources should be open to all, irrespective of their caste.

In 1927, Ambedkar led the Mahad Satyagraha to assert the right of the Dalits. He also founded the Independent Labour Party in 1936 which won fifteen seats in the Legislative Assembly. It was Dr Ambedkar's reputation as a scholar that led to his appointment as free India's first law minister and then the chairman of the Drafting Committee responsible for framing the constitution of free India.

PIVOTAL ROLE AS THE CHAIRMAN

As the chairman of the Drafting Committee of the Constitution, Ambedkar had a tremendous responsibility. He put particular emphasis on the equality of all classes of people and introduced reservation for the scheduled castes and scheduled tribes. After tremendous hard work, Ambedkar was successful in drafting a detailed constitution that safeguarded the integrity and sovereignty of India. The constitution was finally passed on 26 January 1950 and was hailed as the lengthiest written constitution in the world.

DEATH

Dr Ambedkar suffered from diabetes and weak eyesight. He passed away on 6 December 1956. He will always be remembered for his vision and knowledge. One of the greatest Indians, he taught us how to triumph over darkness of the mind and lead the entire humanity towards the liberation of the mind.

DID YOU KNOW?

- He was against Mahatma Gandhi calling the Dalits Harijans.
- He was the first Indian to pursue a doctorate in economics abroad.
- He was awarded the Bharat Ratana posthumously in 1988.

CHARLES DE GAULLE

Charles de Gaulle was one of the greatest Frenchmen to have lived. His memory continues to inspire the people of France even today.

EARLY LIFE

Charles de Gaulle was born on 22 November 1890 in Lille, France. He was born into a devout Roman Catholic family and brought up in a conservative atmosphere, which influenced him throughout his life. He joined the military academy called Saint-Cyr and graduated in 1912.

Gaulle joined the infantry regiment as a lieutenant and proved to be an asset. Besides being an able soldier, Gaulle was also a man with great insight on military strategy which he published in several books. He even received recognition for his services.

GERMAN INVASION AND WORLD WAR II

When Germany invaded France in 1940, the French Army realized that they required the services of Charles de Gaulle even though they had earlier belittled him for having technically advanced tank units. He was given the responsibility of commanding a tank unit, and although he was able to stall the advances of the German Army, the victory was short-lived. His term as the minister of war was also short-lived, as France surrendered to Germany.

He soon fled to England and became an advocate of free France. In one of his radio broadcasts, he made an appeal to the nation that they should not extinguish the flame of French resistance. He became a symbol of the protest against German occupation.

ENTERING POLITICAL LIFE

Gaulle moved to Algeria in 1943 to form the provisional government of France, which annoyed the allies of France. In November 1945, Gaulle was elected without any opposition as the leader of the new French government. A year later, he resigned and formed his own political party but it never achieved political success.

PRESIDENCY

The French government started showing signs of decay in the late 1950s. There was no leader. Gaulle was called to power and elected as the president. Gaulle helped form the new constitution which he called the Fifth French Republic.

During his tenure, Gaulle declared the independence of the French colony, Algeria. Many disapproved his decision but Gaulle stood by his guns. Gaulle was a true nationalist and therefore did not want France to be under the influence of either Britain or the US. In 1966, France pulled out from the North Atlantic Treaty Organization (NATO) and developed its own atom bomb.

DEATH

Gaulle resigned in 1969 and planned to spend the rest of his days writing memoirs. But the following year, he died due to heart failure. With Gaulle's death, France lost a great statesman who had brought back the lost glory of France.

DID YOU KNOW?

- France's largest and Europe's second-largest airport is named after Charles de Gaulle.
- He was taken prisoner in the Battle of Verdun in 1916 by the Germans. He made five failed attempts to escape.
- Franklin D. Roosevelt found Gaulle boastful and biased against the US. In fact, he was so irritated by Gaulle that he did not want to meet him.

CHE GUEVARA

Revolutionary, author, physician, guerrilla leader and diplomat—there are very few people who could come close to the remarkable genius of Che Guevara. Guevara, a key figure of the Cuban Revolution, is now a symbol of rebellion and change.

EARLY LIFE AND BECOMING A REVOLUTIONIST

Born to Ernesto Guevara Lynch and his wife, Celia de la Serna y Llosa, on 14 June 1928 in Rosario, Argentina, Ernesto Guevara was the eldest of five children. Right from his childhood, he was compassionate towards the poor and the deprived.

After graduating from high school, Guevara studied medicine at the University of Buenos Aires. It was during this time that he found his real calling—the desire to reach out to people. He took a year off from his studies and toured South America. During the tour, which he later wrote about and published in a book, *The Motorcycle Diaries*, he was pained to see the working conditions of the people.

Guevara realized that Latin America was unified in its destiny of suffering in the hands of capitalism. He saw how the mobilization of workers led to agrarian reforms and how a US-backed military coup overthrew a revolutionary government. Guevara felt that the old system of political and military power ought to be destroyed and replaced by a system where the ordinary man finds his voice and identity. Meanwhile, he met the Cuban revolutionaries—Fidel Castro and his brother Raúl—who were planning to overthrow Fulgencio Batista's government. Castro invited Guevara to join as a physician but he chose bullets over the medical paraphernalia. This is how he got initiated as a guerrilla. Instead of practising as a doctor, he fought with the Cubans for two years and rose to the level of a rebel army commander.

GUEVARA AS A MINISTER

After the success of the 1959 revolution, Guevara became a Cuban citizen and assumed important positions in the government like the head of the National Bank and the minister of industry. Guevara played a significant role in shaping the economic policy of the country and in bringing various agrarian land reforms.

Guevara did not enjoy the privileges due to a minister; rather, he led an austere and simple life. He used to spend his evenings and weekends in voluntary labour. He travelled across the world representing Cuba. Owing to his discomfort with a position of privilege, Guevara renounced his governmental position and his Cuban citizenship and travelled to Congo in Africa to support the guerrillas. However, he felt like an outsider and left the place. After spending some time in Tanzania, Czechoslovakia and the German Democratic Republic, Guevara returned to Cuba, the place that recognized his contribution and efforts. On his return, he stood against American imperialism and appealed to countries in Asia, Africa and Latin America to strike a deadly blow against the US.

MARTYRDOM

In 1966, he tried to launch a new continental Latin American revolution in Bolivia and led the forces that were rebelling against the government of René Barrientos Ortuño. He failed to gather the support of the local peasantry as they had received land from the government. On 8 October 1967, with the assistance of the US, the Bolivian Army captured Guevara along with his comrades. Guevara was an international figure by then and the Bolivian government did not want to attract much attention, nor give him the scope to escape or undergo trial. The dictator René Barrientos ordered his prompt execution and the Bolivian forces shot him on 9 October 1967. Yet, even after decades, Guevara does not fail to inspire people to place broader interests of society over narrow personal gains.

DID YOU KNOW?

- In Rosario city, Guevara's birthplace, there is a twelve-foot bronze statue of Guevara created using 75,000 keys donated by Che supporters from around the world.
- Before 1959, Cuba had a literacy rate of around 60 per cent. When Che took over, he built schools and trained teachers, and as a result, the literacy rate increased to 96 per cent.
- His diary entries during his motorcycle trip have also been made into a movie called *The Motorcycle Diaries* in 2004.

DALAI LAMA

The Dalai Lama is a symbol of peace and infinite patience. In addition to being the spiritual leader of Tibet, he is also the face of political activism of his country.

EARLY LIFE

Lhamo Thondup was born on 6 July 1935 in Taktser, to the northeast of Tibet, to a humble peasant family. At the age of two, he was located by the religious officials and recognized as the reincarnation of the 13th Dalai Lama, Thubten Gyatso. He was renamed Tenzin Gyatso and was recognized as the 14th Dalai Lama. Dalai Lama literally translates to 'Ocean Teacher', which means a teacher with the spiritual depth of an ocean.

EDUCATION AND POLITICAL CONTROL

Gyatso began his religious education at the age of six. Besides religious learning, his teaching also consisted of Tibetan art and culture, medicine, Sanskrit and Buddhist philosophy. In 1950, at the young age of fifteen, Gyatso was made the Dalai Lama and given all political control of Tibet. However, his governance could not continue for long, as the People's Republic of China invaded Tibet in the same year. The Dalai Lama failed, despite making several attempts to reconcile with China. Fearing an assassination, he and several of his followers escaped from Tibet and entered India through Arunachal Pradesh in 1959. He established an alternative government in Dharamshala, Himachal Pradesh, India. Since then, he has been in exile.

LIFE IN EXILE

The Dalai Lama has been making various attempts to establish a Tibetan autonomous state within the Republic of China. However, the constitution drafted by him in 1963, recognizing the democracy of Tibet and the rights of the Tibetans, was a failure.

In 1987, the Five Point Peace Plan was conceived to reconcile with China. The Dalai Lama demanded that Tibet should be allowed to maintain its own identity, without interference from China, and China would be responsible for Tibet's defence and foreign policies. This plea was also negated by the Chinese government.

The Dalai Lama officially retired as the political leader of Tibet in 2011. He also signed a law which allowed the country to officially elect a democratic official, thereby ending the 350-year-old tradition where the Dalai Lama was not only the spiritual but also the political leader.

SPIRITUAL LEADER

The Dalai Lama has followers and admirers across the world. He tours the world, preaching to people about the teachings of Buddhism. His main teachings are compassion, love and realizing inner happiness. Following the tradition of Bodhisattva, he has dedicated his life to the cause of humanity.

The Dalai Lama has attended many interfaith services and has always shown respect for all the religions of the world. He has also made a plea towards an urgent need for understanding the environment for human sustenance.

MESSENGER OF PEACE

The Nobel Peace Prize which was given to him in 1989 was a way of acknowledging the tremendous strength exhibited by this monk who faced all his problems with a smile. Such souls are a way of reiterating the fact that there is still hope for humanity.

DID YOU KNOW?

- While escaping from Lhasa to India, the Dalai Lama took the guise of a soldier and was even given a gun as a prop.
- Although the Dalai Lama is an international figure, his pictures have been banned in Tibet by the Chinese government.
- The Dalai Lama has a number of hobbies, his favourite being meditating, gardening and repairing watches.

DAVID CAMERON

David Cameron, the prime minister of England from 2010 to 2016, was a leader who led from the front. He came with a promise of rapid express development at a time of great economic crisis.

EARLY LIFE

David Cameron was born into a well-to-do family on 9 October 1966. He is a descendant of King William IV. His father was a stockbroker and his mother a retired justice of the peace. Cameron attended the elite Heatherdown prep school and then went on to attend Eton College at the age of thirteen. Cameron graduated in 1988 from Oxford University. After graduation, he joined the Conservative Party's Research Department as an advisor. Then, Cameron joined a media company as the director of corporate affairs.

JOINING POLITICS

Cameron started his political pursuits and won a parliamentary seat in 2001 as a representative of the Conservative Party. He soon emerged as the leader of the party. The conservatives had been losing all elections and were obviously apprehensive about the elections of 2005. Many were skeptical of giving the leadership to an inexperienced person like Cameron, but he was a charismatic leader and therefore it was expected that he would be able to bring in change.

Cameron soon soared as a brand manager of the Conservative Party. Cameron built his image of being a nice person and not an unsympathetic one from the upper class. David Cameron was an untested leader and the Conservatives were not sorry for their choice of leadership because he became the prime minister of England in 2010. When Cameron assumed office, there were some serious problems in the country. He inherited a deficit economy but worked relentlessly to reduce government debt.

Cameron took the momentous decision to form a coalition government with the liberal democrats.

CONTRIBUTION

Cameron was a suave politician and he charmed everyone. He issued some spending cuts in health services and education. He took a very strong stand on immigration and opined that immigration should be subject to annual limits. This decision got a mixed response.

Cameron developed friendly relations with foreign countries. He visited Paris, Berlin, Russia and the US to form friendly ties.

These relations were crucial to forming a joint European Union (EU) negotiation. Britain has played a key role under him in the Copenhagen climate change meeting and in framing the global financial regulations.

Cameron also contained unemployment to a great extent. But Cameron's most important achievement is perhaps the rebirth of the Conservative Party which might have gone into oblivion had it not tasted success under Cameron's flagship. He won elections again in 2016 with a majority. In the wake of Britain voting to opt out of the EU, Cameron resigned from his office in 2016. Cameron will always be known as a champion of democracy, happiness, compassion and humanitarian values.

DID YOU KNOW?

- David Cameron is also a columnist and writes for *The Guardian*.
- At forty-four years, Cameron was the youngest prime minister of Britain since 1812.
- Cameron had an internet TV channel, 'Webcameron', covering him exclusively from the kitchen to wherever he went.

DILMA ROUSSEFF

Known as the Mother of Brazil, Dilma Rousseff's journey from being a guerrilla to the first elected president of her country is fascinating.

EARLY LIFE

Born on 14 December 1947, Dilma Rousseff's father was an immigrant from Bulgaria and a lawyer, and her mother was a school teacher. Dilma showed an early interest in politics. When in high school, she joined the party called Worker's Politics, which later on became the National Liberation Command. She was also influenced by Marxist ideas and believed that armed struggle was the only way to bring in change.

BECOMING A GUERRILLA

In 1970, Dilma participated in an uprising of sailors against a military coup and was arrested for three years, even having to endure torture. Her arrest was a deciding point of her life. She resumed her education after her release and graduated in economics in 1977, and became actively involved in politics as well.

Dilma also worked as the editor of the newspaper, *The Piquet*, which advocated Marxist views. Eventually, she became involved in underground activities and, between 1964 and 1985, she participated in armed conflict against military dictatorship.

POLITICS AND PRESIDENCY

Over time, she became affiliated with Lula da Silva, the would-be president of the country. Dilma soon quit her government job in 2002 and devoted herself to campaigning for Lula. When Lula took over the office of the president in 2003, Dilma was selected as the president of the Foundation of Economics and Statistics of the state of Rio Grande do Sul. Later, Dilma became the secretary of Mines, Energy and Communications for the same state. With the help of mentoring from Lula, Dilma Rousseff ran for the presidential elections in 2010. Her agenda during the campaign focused on economic stability, poverty eradication, removing unemployment and bringing in reforms in both political and tax matters. On 1 January 2011, Dilma won with a huge margin and was sworn in as the president of Brazil.

Dilma lived up to the expectations of the people, and her foreign policy stressed on human rights violation rampant during the military rule. In 2011, she signed the Landmark Law which established a truth commission to investigate the violation of human rights. This strengthened the position of Brazil in the global arena.

Dilma also grew popular as a great economist. She pushed for the completion of a number of hydroelectric dam projects, and encouraged Brazilians to be self-reliant, and produce their own goods.

ACCUSATIONS AND IMPEACHMENT

Despite the growth Dilma brought into her country, she and her cabinet faced allegations of corruption. In the midst of this trial, the growth of Brazil's economy came down. The country saw many street protests that disrupted the entire government machinery. Dilma said that she was a victim of a coup, meant to prevent the economic liberalization of Brazil and stop the investigators from reaching the corrupt. Dilma Rousseff was suspended and Michel Temer became the acting president.

DID YOU KNOW?

- Dilma was the first female president of Brazil.
- Dilma democratized the electricity sector through the programme 'Light for All', which made electricity available even in rural areas.
- Dilma was diagnosed with cancer after she announced her presidential candidacy, but she defeated it.

DONALD J. TRUMP

The charismatic Donald J. Trump is the 45th president of the US. His strength doesn't lie in being a successful businessman, TV personality or a statesman but in his capability to steer through any problem in life.

EARLY LIFE

Donald John Trump was the fourth child of Frederick Trump and Mary MacLeod Trump. As a student, he excelled both in academics and sports. After his graduation from the Wharton School of Finance at the University of Pennsylvania, he joined his father in his business.

BUSINESS AND POLITICS

Trump had learnt a lot from his father and desired to establish his own business. The skyline of Manhattan beckoned him. He started buying property whose owner was in distress, and then turned the place around. He bought and renovated hotels, and soon became a flourishing businessman. He suffered losses in 1989 due to poor business decisions, and was almost on the verge of bankruptcy. But he soon catapulted back on the road to success. His greatest strength was that he knew what to sell and what people wanted. He marketed his name on numerous products like Trump Financial, Trump Sales and Leasing, Trump Entrepreneur Initiative, Trump restaurants, and many more.

In 2000, he expressed his wish to have a political career but became vocal about his political views only after 2010. Because of these, and his open denouncement of Barack Obama, Trump began to be noticed in the world of conservative politics. Finally, in June 2015, Trump announced his presidential candidacy. His adage—Make America Great Again—garnered a lot of interest and support among the Americans. Some of his promises were to create millions of jobs for the Americans, cut taxes and stop illegal immigration as well as government lobbyism.

PRESIDENT OF AMERICA

On 8 November 2016, Donald Trump defeated Hillary Clinton and took over the office of the president. He brought in many radical changes as was promised by him—withdrawing of Obama care, changing some federal legislations, to name a few. The illegal crossing of the borders went down significantly after he took to office.

His decision to launch missiles against Syria in the wake of a chemical attack was applauded back home.

In his pursuance of the 'America First' agenda, he has withdrawn from the Trans-Pacific partnership negotiations, the Paris agreement on climatic change and the Iran nuclear deal.

DID YOU KNOW?

- Trump owned 14,000 apartments by the time he was twenty-seven years old.
- Trump is a germaphobe, which means he is very conscious of cleanliness. Therefore, he hates shaking hands with others.
- Trump is very conscious of the short length of his fingers.

DWIGHT D. EISENHOWER

Dwight Eisenhower's stature has seldom been matched with the other key players of not only his country but the entire world. The 34th president of the US, Eisenhower, was a man of great military prowess, as well as political genius.

EARLY LIFE

Dwight David Eisenhower was born on 14 October 1890 in Aibeline, Kansas in a humble and religious family and knew what it meant to be poor. As a child, he was always active and happy. Although he excelled in baseball, it was football that he loved. Eisenhower was brought up with a feeling of patriotism, dignity of hard work and religious guidance.

JOINING MILITARY ACADEMY

At the age of twenty, Eisenhower left home to join the military academy. He began his march into history as a cadet. After his graduation in 1915, he was commissioned as a second lieutenant. World War I gave him the opportunity to command a tank training centre where he prepared troops for their overseas duty.

MILITARY CAREER

Eisenhower graduated in 1915, and by then he had earned his name for his service in the First World War. He was sent on an assignment to France to prepare a guidebook on American battlefields in Europe. After returning to the US in 1940, he became the chief of staff of the Third Army that was coming up as the troop with knowledge about the latest war manoeuvers yet witnessed by the troops. He was soon promoted to the position of a brigadier. The bombing of Pearl Harbour by the Japanese was a turning point not only for the fate of the nation but also for Eisenhower.

Eisenhower was made a general in 1943 and given the prime responsibility of initiating the allied invasion of Nazi-occupied Europe. This was pivotal to the world history as he led the crusade that liberated Europe. He was given a hero's welcome in the US and was made the chief of the US Army.

ENTERING POLITICS

Eisenhower retired from the army in 1952 but was requested by the then president, Harry S. Truman, to take command of the North Atlantic Treaty Organization (NATO) forces in Europe to combat communist aggression. Meanwhile, Truman's popularity was slackening, and thus Eisenhower was approached to run for president.

Eisenhower took over as the president of the US on 4 November 1952. His victories as the president are numerous.

Eisenhower contributed immensely towards building the infrastructure of the US. The interstate highway system was developed by him, and about 41,000 miles of roads were constructed across the country. The president also strengthened the national security programme, and increased the minimum wage. Education and health were given a lot of attention as well.

Despite his military background, Eisenhower always believed in maintaining peace with the other nations of the world. The military was undoubtedly an important instrument for foreign policy but it was always treated as the last resort. He believed that the president should be capable enough to resolve the issues himself, without seeking military aid. He resisted going to war with many countries to maintain peace.

DEATH AND LEGACY

Eisenhower is undoubtedly one of the best presidents of the US because he understood the needs of the people. He knew that without stability, the US could never emerge as a strong power in the world. Post presidency, he wrote several books and spent a peaceful life at his farm. However, he fell prey to his long illness and passed away on 28 March 1969.

DID YOU KNOW?

- Eisenhower was against the dropping of atomic bombs in Hiroshima and Nagasaki.
- He took up painting as a hobby when he was around 58. He made at least 250 paintings.
- He banished the White House squirrels because they used to ruin his putting green for golf by stuffing them with acorns and walnuts.

ELIZABETH I

A woman of grace and high self-esteem, Elizabeth I, the queen of England, was the most famous of all English monarchs. Her biggest contribution was her ability to bring in peace in the internal turmoil-torn England.

EARLY LIFE
Elizabeth I was born to King Henry VIII and his second wife Anne Boleyn on 7 September 1533 in Greenwich, England. She lost her mother at an early age of two. Elizabeth received education fit for a princess, and she excelled in music and the arts.

Elizabeth learnt five different languages, read philosophy and history and loved writing. After the demise of her father, her brother King Edward VI assumed the throne. However, his reign was short-lived and eventually Elizabeth became the queen in 1558.

QUEEN ELIZABETH
Life was not easy for Elizabeth as she always had to be on her guard for any kind of plotting and rebellion. The two pressing issues were religious divide between the Catholics and the Protestants and the war with the French. She was able to tackle both issues skilfully.

Queen Elizabeth came up with a common book of prayer for everyone and thus satisfied both the factions of Christianity. She said that 'there is one Jesus Christ' and 'the rest is a dispute over trifles'. She also ended the war with France and was successful in avoiding conflicts with other European powers for quite some time. In 1588, by defeating the superpower Spain, she established England's supremacy over the naval route.

England, under the rule of Queen Elizabeth, was a land of opulence and opportunities. The economy grew fast, and various art forms, fashion and theatre flourished. It was during Queen

Elizabeth's time that the plays of the famous playwrights like William Shakespeare and Christopher Marlowe became popular.

THE REIGN OF QUEEN ELIZABETH

Queen Elizabeth was an accomplished ruler and knew that a country can scale heights only through all-round development. She, therefore, encouraged new scientific thinking and many important thinkers like Sir Francis Bacon and Dr John Dee emerged in this period. She travelled across her kingdom and ensured that her subjects were living in a good condition.

The queen established what was popularly known as 'poor laws', which was an excellent framework to help the poor and the needy. Her public relations and the art of rhetoric were par excellence. She was a great statesman and had the rare ability to choose the best advisors, but was also able to maintain her integrity and not be dominated by any of them.

DEATH AND SUCCESSOR

Queen Elizabeth I breathed her last on 24 March 1603. As she had never married, she did not have an heir. During the last days of her life, she fell so ill that speech failed her. She could just point to the crown on her head when asked who her successor should be. They assumed that she meant King James VI of Scotland was to succeed the throne because he was the most eligible to succeed her, owing to his great-grandmother Margaret Tudor being the elder sister of King Henry VIII. Moreover, Queen Elizabeth was the last descendant of Henry VIII. Her success as a ruler is unparalleled in history and so, in her honour, an entire epoch is dubbed as 'The Elizabethan Age'.

DID YOU KNOW?

- She was very fashion-conscious and was said to have around 2,000 pairs of gloves.
- The efficiency with which Queen Elizabeth ruled earned her reign to be termed as the 'Golden Age'.
- The Queen had a firm belief in astrology and always consulted astrologers before taking a major decision or even scheduling events.

ELLEN JOHNSON SIRLEAF

E llen Johnson Sirleaf, a daring and courageous lady, was the 24th president of Liberia who left an indelible mark in a male-dominated world and changed the history of her country.

EARLY YEARS

Ellen was born on 28 October 1938 in Monrovia, Liberia to Jahmale Carmel Johnson. Since childhood, she nurtured the dream of either becoming the president of her country or holding a high office. Ellen loved to play football and climb trees. Her outspoken nature always set her apart. She spoke of equality, a value instilled in her by her parents. After her graduation in Liberia, Ellen went to the US for higher education.

ENTERING POLITICS

Ellen returned to Liberia and served as an assistant minister of finance in President William Tolbert's administration. Her fiery speech attracted the attention of the Liberian Chamber of Commerce.

A year after the president's assassination in 1980, and execution of most of his cabinet ministers, Ellen was amongst the lucky four who survived. Ellen was sentenced to ten years' imprisonment for speaking against the regime, but due to international pressure, her term was reduced to less than a year.

CIVIL WAR

She left for the US in 1986 in the face of death threats and worked to attract international attention towards her country. Meanwhile, a civil war broke out in Liberia. Charles Taylor rebelled against the then President Samuel Doe, who was overthrown in 1990 by Prince Yormie Johnson, and later killed in the same year.

Thirty years of war had destroyed every inch of Liberia and all progress came to a halt. In 1994, Liberia witnessed a change, and female activists emerged in great numbers. They were up against the mass and wanton killings. Peace negotiations finally led to a ceasefire in 1996, and Ellen Sirleaf also returned to Liberia.

PRESIDENT OF LIBERIA

General elections were held in 1997. Many people were not sure that Ellen would return, as she and Charles could not see eye to eye. But she braved all opposition and joined the Unity Party since it did not have any candidate. This way she could run for president. Charles Taylor won the election and he was made the president.

But peace did not last for long. Liberia was attacked by a rebel group in 1999. After the conflict raged for four years, women activists, including Ellen, convinced the rebel leaders and Charles Taylor to negotiate peace. Charles went into exile and the country required a new government. Finally, with the spirit and strength of female activists, Ellen became the president in 2006.

CONTRIBUTION

With the coming of Sirleaf to power, a new era of change arrived along with the hope for better conditions for women and children. Better education and freedom of speech have been the two things she has worked for since the beginning.

The Sirleaf Market Women's Fund gives traders business management and literacy training. Children have better opportunities, and women no longer shy away from politics. She started a programme ensuring free and compulsory education for children up to class nine. Ellen also travelled across the country trying to motivate people and making them aware of their rights. Today, with a transformed Liberia, Ellen Sirleaf has rightfully earned the sobriquet, Africa's Iron Lady.

DID YOU KNOW?

- Sirleaf got the Nobel Peace Prize in 2011.
- She studied economics and public policy at Harvard University.
- She worked as an influential economist for World Bank, Citibank and other international institutions.

EMMELINE PANKHURST

An iconic lady and political activist, Emmeline Pankhurst transformed the lives of women through her suffragette movement.

EARLY LIFE AND EDUCATION

Emmeline Goulden was born in July 1858 in Manchester, England. She was the eldest of ten children. Although women couldn't vote at that time, Emmeline grew up in a family where women were considered no less than men in any aspect. All of them advocated the right of a woman to vote. She completed her studies in Paris and returned to Manchester.

ENTRY INTO POLITICS

Although Emmeline got introduced to the subject of women's voting rights through her mother, her barrister husband, Richard Pankhurst, lent active support to women's suffrage and other causes. After her marriage, Emmeline became active in politics and began voicing her protests for not allowing women to vote. She was an impressive speaker, and soon she started being acknowledged by people.

Emmeline formed the Women's Social and Political Union (WSPU), a women's group that demanded voting rights for women. All her three daughters actively supported her cause. Her children were imprisoned several times and they also founded the magazine 'Vote for Women', which voiced the opinion of women.

POLITICAL ACTIVISM

Women from all walks of life, such as factory workers, authors, teachers, actresses and many more, joined the suffrage movement. They held many demonstrations where Emmeline demanded the government to either give voting rights to women or kill them. When women found that they were unable to exert adequate pressure on the government, they began vandalizing public property and got arrested. In 1909, they even started hunger strikes and demanded to be recognized as political prisoners and not criminals. The prison authorities were left with no choice but to force-feed the suffragettes.

Emmeline was given a nine-month sentence for throwing a stone at the prime minister's residence. She was in and out of prison several times. This led to the 'Cat and Mouse Act', allowing suffragettes to be out once they were unwell, and rearrested after they regained health.

Emmeline regularly visited the US for raising funds for the party. On 18 November 1910, WSPU organized a mass protest by 300 women who marched to the Houses of Parliament. Women were injured as they were attacked with stones, rotten eggs etc. by the police. The day came to be known as Black Friday.

FIRST WORLD WAR AND SUFFRAGETTE RIGHTS

During the First World War, Emmeline's demand that all women suffragettes be allowed to contribute to the country in the times of crisis helped them as the government began considering suffragette rights to women.

Although in 1918, the government gave limited voting rights to women over the age of thirty and having private property, voting rights of men were from the age of twenty-one. Emmeline continued with her fight, and on 4 June 1928, she breathed her last.

CONTRIBUTION

Emmeline gave a new lease of life to women. The suffragette movement was the only movement in the history of Great Britain that was won by violence.

DID YOU KNOW?

- Emmeline invented the idea of putting letter bombs into letter boxes to cause unrest.
- The suffragettes were trained in martial arts to protect important leaders against the police.
- Emmeline sold her house in 1907 and moved from place to place, delivering inspiring speeches.

F.W. DE KLERK

F.W. de Klerk was the man who ended apartheid and ushered in democracy in South Africa.

EARLY LIFE

Frederik Willem de Klerk was born on 18 March 1936 in Johannesburg, South Africa. He was born into a political family with both his father and grandfather serving as high officials. He completed his schooling from Krugersdorp and graduated in law from Potchefstroom University in 1958. Klerk started practising law and opened a law firm in the small town called Vereeniging in South Africa. Around this time, he also started taking interest in the politics of South Africa and was elected to the parliament for the National Party.

CAREER IN POLITICS

Klerk was known for his conservative approach and upheld the apartheid system. He held several ministerial positions, including minister of Post and Telecommunications, Sport and recreation, Mines, amongst others, during President Pieter Willem Botha's term. His career took a different turn when he succeeded P.W. Botha as the leader of the National Party. In September 1989, Klerk was elected as the president.

PRESIDENT OF SOUTH AFRICA

Klerk's selection as the president was not met favourably by the people of South Africa, as he was white. The members of the African National Congress (ANC) felt that he was no different from his predecessors, and protest marches were held against him, to which, surprisingly, Klerk did not object.

On assuming power, Klerk started doing things which gave indication to the people that he was different from his predecessors.

Klerk ordered the release of many elderly anti-apartheid prisoners and went on to accept that apartheid was morally incorrect. Klerk embraced and even made others in his party embrace the vision of 'One United South Africa'. He proposed to ban all types of discrimination—racial, ethnic, gender, religious, etc. Klerk even made changes in the constitution to uphold the laws of equality. However, he faced a tough time convincing the whites to give up their power and share it with the blacks.

ESTABLISHING ANTI-APARTHEID GOVERNMENT
Klerk met Nelson Mandela while the latter was a prisoner. Mandela was released on 11 February 1990 along with other political prisoners. Klerk also removed the ban from African National Congress and joined hands with Nelson Mandela to bring changes in the country. Although both had disagreements, they accepted each other's integrity. Klerk had high regard for Mandela and both created a common ground for successful negotiations to take place.

Nelson Mandela was elected as the first black president of South Africa in May 1994 and Klerk became his deputy. Mandela and Klerk started with the construction of the new nation, and together they ended the scourge of apartheid in South Africa.

RETIREMENT
After his retirement from politics, Klerk set up the Global Leadership Foundation, a non-profitable organization of people with important positions in various governments across the world, with the primary function to offer advice to heads of state. He encourages leaders across the world for the continuance of democracy despite all hardships.

DID YOU KNOW?

- Klerk was called a traitor by the white people because he wanted to give more power to the blacks.
- Klerk and Mandela were the co-recipients of the Nobel Peace Prize for bringing reforms in South Africa.
- He has been awarded with the highest South African honour bestowed on citizens and foreigners–the Order of Mapungubwe.

FIDEL CASTRO

Fidel Castro is an unforgettable name in the history of the world. His identity is intertwined with the identity of Cuba, which he wanted to be self-reliant.

EARLY LIFE

Fidel Castro was born in a sugar plantation in Biran on 13 August 1926. His father was an immigrant from Spain and was a fairly successful farmer. Castro's father was a progressive man and ensured the education of his children. After completing school, Castro entered the School of Law at the University of Havana.

Castro was passionate about changing the condition of the Cubans, which made him participate in various agitations staged by the students. Castro's campaigns against American imperialism made him a charismatic leader, and in 1947, he joined the party of the Cuban people.

EARLY POLITICAL CAREER

Castro immersed himself into politics after getting his law degree and vowed to expose the corruption of the Fulgencio Batista government. In doing so, Castro was drawn towards the ideas of Marxism. The plight of the poor moved him and he realized that simply exposing corrupt politicians would not be enough; he had to change the system wherein the bourgeoisie dictated terms to the government. He started visiting the villages and witnessed the racial discrimination existing there, which further intensified his desire to fight for the exploited class.

Castro began his law practice and started helping poor Cubans to stand up for their rights. He organized a parallel government against that of Batista's, and started mobilizing groups. Castro named the rebellion the 26th of July Movement in 1953. Although the rebellion failed, a new leader emerged in Cuba and he formed a revolutionary group.

Despite being imprisoned, Fidel developed strategies to oust the dictatorship of Batista. He made certain significant agrarian reforms. Finally, the Batista government crumbled, and Fidel Castro was sworn in as the prime minister on 16 February 1959.

CASTRO AS THE PRIME MINISTER

He initiated several reforms resulting in the nationalization of factories and plantations. The lower class saw in him a source of their liberation from hard-grinding poverty and deprivation. Across the country, Castro opened schools where education was combined with productive activity and health centres which offered free medical aid. Vaccination was administered to reduce infant mortality drastically.

Castro's plans also included developing sanitation and safe drinking water, housing for the homeless and the destitute and building extensive roads across Cuba. He also helped the disabled and the deprived, and provided electricity to households.

In his desire to reach out to people, Castro used radio and television channels. However, he started losing his popularity among the middle class as they felt that they were being deprived of the benefits. Many middle-class people migrated to the US, causing immense brain drain in Cuba.

BIRTH OF THE SOCIALIST CUBA

Castro had many supporters in Cuba but there was also a large faction that was against him. In April 1961, many exiled Cubans, who had been trained by the Central Investigation Agency, invaded Cuba to overthrow the Castro government but failed. To counter American imperialism in Latin America and Africa, Castro formed the Cuba Communist Party. Cuba's ally, the Soviet Union, compelled an angry US not to invade Cuba.

Cuba gradually emerged as a socialist state that ended its elections in 1962. A new constitution was formulated and Castro was declared the president of both the council of states and the council of ministers. He resigned due to prolonged illness in 2008.

DID YOU KNOW?

- Castro used to go to bed at around 3 or 4 a.m. He liked to meet foreign diplomats at this odd hour as he wanted to have an upper hand in the discussion.
- He survived more than 600 assassination attempts.
- He did not have any liking for music but was a great lover of sports.

FRANKLIN D. ROOSEVELT

Franklin Delano Roosevelt, the 32nd president of the US, was a beacon of hope who brought his country together at a time of despair.

EARLY LIFE

Franklin Delano Roosevelt was born on 30 January 1882 in Hyde Park, New York, to wealthy parents who had made their fortune in trade and real estate. Roosevelt's mother was a doting parent who tutored him at home. In 1900, when Roosevelt was nine, his world was shattered when his father died from a heart attack.

At Harvard, he was an average student but succeeded in winning popularity because of his oratory skills and energy.

ENTERING POLITICS

Roosevelt developed interest in politics and won a seat as a democrat in 1910. In 1912, Roosevelt supported the presidential candidate, Woodrow Wilson, and was appointed the assistant secretary of the navy. He held that position for seven years, emerging as a national leader.

Roosevelt had the secret desire to be the president of the US. He idolized Theodore Roosevelt. Eventually, he decided to run for a US senate seat which he lost. But this did not deter him from aiming for higher posts. At the age of thirty-eight, he was the youngest to run for vice president, but here, too, he was a failure.

PRESIDENCY

In 1928, Roosevelt was elected as the governor of New York. This victory gave him a lot of confidence and he decided to participate in the presidential elections, which he won. On 4 March 1933, Roosevelt was elected the US president. The US was in great economic depression during that time. In his famous inaugural address, he said, 'This great nation will endure as it has endured...The only thing we have to fear is fear itself.'

He was a president with earnestness who wanted to take the US to a new level. Roosevelt's first 100 days in office were momentous. He addressed American citizens through radio broadcasts and soon became a household name in the US. He was a missile of energy that brought reforms in every sector such as agriculture, public administration and many more. He also provided economic relief for workers and farmers, and created jobs for the unemployed. He regulated wages and prices. By 1935, the economy of the country started showing signs of recovery.

SECOND, THIRD AND FOURTH INNINGS

Roosevelt was elected as the president four times. He curtailed government spending to boost the economy. His social programmes reinvented the role played by the government in a person's life. It was during his time that the US emerged as a world leader. Initially, the US was neutral about wars, but later it participated in them and even came out in support of Britain. The US did this to contain Germany which it thought may win the war. Roosevelt breathed his last on 12 April 1945. The people of the US poured out into the streets to express their grief.

DID YOU KNOW?

- Roosevelt's wife Eleanor Roosevelt was the niece of President Theodore Roosevelt.
- Roosevelt loved his pet dog, Fala, so much that it accompanied him on his trips. Fala was buried alongside the president.
- Roosevelt was afraid of the number thirteen. He never had food at a table that would seat thirteen people.

GEORGE W. BUSH JR

George Walker Bush, the 43rd president of the US was a man who declared war against terrorism and was resolute about winning it.

EARLY LIFE

George W. Bush was born on 6 July 1946 in New Haven, Connecticut. He was born into a well-to-do family. His father moved to west Texas and started an oil business. After the death of his young sister, Robin, George took it upon himself to take care of everyone to come out of the grief. George was also a popular kid in the neighbourhood.

The Bush family moved to Houston in 1959 and George Bush enrolled in Phillips Academy in Massachusetts, a boarding school for boys. He graduated from Yale University with a degree in history and later enlisted himself in the Texas National Guard and flew jet fighters on weekends for five years. His father was also a decorated pilot during World War II. Bush got his master's degree in MBA from Harvard University in 1975.

EARLY CAREER

Just like his father, George set out for the oil fields of Texas to begin his career. He set up his own company called Arbusto but did not achieve the same level of success as his father. He eventually decided to join politics and ran for the Congressional seat in west Texas, but lost his first election. In 1988, George was invited by his father, Senior Bush, who was contesting the presidential elections, to join him as an advisor of the campaign committee. He returned to Texas after Senior Bush became the president. George's friend offered him the opportunity to invest in the Texas Rangers baseball team there. It was a dream come true for him and he became the team's managing general partner.

ENTERING POLITICS

After the re-election loss of Senior Bush, George and his brother decided to run for Governor—Jeb from Florida and George from Texas. George was able to impress everyone with his easy and amicable style and was elected as the governor in 1995. Thereafter, George went on to be elected governor for four successive terms. He lowered the taxes and promoted educational reform. He also passed a tough law for juvenile criminals.

PRESIDENCY

In 2000, George became the president of the US. As president, George Bush paid utmost attention to domestic issues like education, tax relief, social security, etc. He did not pay much attention to foreign affairs. However, after the 9/11 attacks on the twin towers in New York by al-Qaeda terrorists, Bush found his real mission and declared war against terrorism. George promised the people of the US that he would avenge the people who had caused such catastrophes in the country. On 7 October 2001, George Bush attacked Afghanistan for harbouring Laden. The US intelligence agencies began to arrest and detain al-Qaeda terrorists around the world. Bush then turned his attention to Saddam Hussein, the ruler of Iraq. He wanted to disarm the nation. He became a very popular leader and this resulted in a sweeping victory in the 2002 mid-term presidential elections. Under Bush's supervision, the US invaded Iraq and defeated it.

Bush was sworn in for the second term on 20 January 2005. He championed the cause of bringing in a change in the Middle East by initiating peace talks between Israel and Palestine, and accomplishing the first democratic election in Iraq.

DID YOU KNOW?

- George Bush was given the title the 'Vacation President' as he took 900 days of leave in his tenure of eight years.
- Bush's favourite food includes peanut butter, grilled cheese sandwiches, honey sandwiches, etc.
- In 2005, Bush was nearly assassinated in Georgia when a grenade was thrown at him. Miraculously, the grenade did not explode.

GEORGE WASHINGTON

George Washington, the first American president, was a true embodiment of the new American republic. He was the only president who was unanimously elected, in the true sense of the term.

EARLY YEARS

Washington was born on 22 February 1732, in Westmoreland County, Virginia. Not much is known about his childhood except that his great-grandfather had migrated to Virginia from England. Virginia was then a province of the British Empire. Coming from a modest family, Washington grew up in an ordinary neighbourhood. He lost his father at the tender age of eleven and his formal education ended when he was fourteen. By the age of seventeen, he was working as the surveyor of the Blue Badge Mountains. Washington's half-brother, whom he admired a lot, died in July 1752 and left behind a fortune for him, and he became the head of one of his prominent estates.

MILITARY CAREER

During the Cold War that ensued between England and France, Washington was appointed as the major of the Virginia militia to teach the civilians about war. He was sent to warn the French to remove themselves from the land that belonged to Britain. Washington was unsuccessful in this and later went with his small force to attack the French. But even this was unsuccessful. Washington fought bravely and was later made the commander of all Virginia troops. He retired from the Virginia regiment in December 1758 and realized that he would only be able to make a mark as a civilian.

BIRTH OF A REVOLUTIONARY

Washington found that despite great produce in the fields, the profits were marginal and the major portion went to Britain. Thus, the British were taking raw materials from them and selling their finished products at higher prices. Washington decided that instead of the commercial crop, tobacco, he would grow grains and achieve economic independence for the US as this move would make the country self-reliant.

As he realized that the US required political independence to prosper, he called for a total boycott of British goods and very soon he was appointed the commander-in-chief of the colonial forces to fight the British. Washington's military experience and legislative knowledge made him the best choice to wage the war of American independence.

AMERICAN INDEPENDENCE

The war of independence lasted for eight years during which Washington's troops were underfed, under-dressed and even under-supplied. During these years, Washington constantly tried to uplift the morale of his soldiers and kept demanding authorities for more supplies. Washington was brilliant in the field; he led charges into the thick of a battlefield, yet dexterously escaped all shots and attacks. Finally, on 19 October 1781, the British surrendered and the US became independent.

FIRST PRESIDENT OF THE US

After independence, the moot question was what sort of governance the US should have. Washington refused this proposition that he should be made king, and was unanimously chosen as the first president of the US. The first thing that Washington did was to establish a formal body of government.

Washington realized the responsibility on his shoulders and he knew he was paving the way for future presidents of the US. When the constitution was formulated, it gave Washington the power to appoint judges, cabinet ministers, public ministers, etc. Washington appointed these officials on the basis of their deservability and employed people from all regions, thus laying the foundation of an inclusive culture.

Washington served two terms as the president, and in both terms, he was unanimously elected. He refused to run for the third term and retired to Mount Vernon, taking care of his plantation. Washington breathed his last on 14 December 1799.

DID YOU KNOW?

- Washington suffered from many ailments unlike the other US presidents till date.
- He had written approximately 20,000 letters in his lifetime.
- He loved dogs and had around thirty as pets, giving them unusual names like Tartar, Truelove and Sweet Lips.

GIRIJA PRASAD KOIRALA

Having served as the prime minister at four different times, the iconic Girija Prasad Koirala has earned the awe and respect of not only the Nepalese but also of people across the world.

EARLY LIFE

Girija Prasad Koirala was born on 4 July 1924 in Saharsa, Bihar. His father Krishna Prasad Koirala was in exile in India during that time. Being an admirer of Mahatma Gandhi, Koirala frequently sought exile in India. Koirala comes from an eminent family of politicians, and his two elder brothers were also prime ministers of Nepal. Koirala completed his education from Kirori Mal College in New Delhi.

ENTERING POLITICS

Koirala's political career began when he initiated the Biratnagar jute mill labour strike in 1947, which soon turned into a nationwide protest against the regime. He formed the Nepal Mazdoor Congress in 1948 and worked to unify the labourers to protest against exploitation. Unimpressed, the king imprisoned Koirala in 1960, for seven years, after which he was exiled to India. Despite this, Koirala returned to Nepal in 1979 and became the secretary general of the Nepali Congress. There, he led the famous People Movement which shook the very foundations of monarchy and established constitutional democracy in Nepal.

PRIME MINISTER

Nepal had its first parliamentary elections in 1991. The Nepali Congress won the elections and Girija Prasad Koirala was selected as the leader of the party. He eventually became the prime minister.

Koirala opened universities and institutes across the country and liberalized education policies. Koirala also opened hospitals and cancer institutes, which helped him become a popular leader who symbolized change and growth. Koirala's second and third term witnessed the rise of the Maoists of the Communist Party of Nepal. In 2001, a civil war broke out in Nepal, and Koirala had to resign.

FOURTH AND FIFTH TERM

Nepal was a highly unstable country, and since Koirala personified stability, he was elected again and again to lead the country. Meanwhile, the Nepali people rose against the rule of King Gyanendra, and demanded that the king declare Nepal a republic. This led to the Loktantra Andolan in 2006. The House of Representatives was reinstated, and Koirala was elected as the prime minister for the fourth term.

The new government stripped all powers of the king and curtailed the power of the military by bringing the army under civilian control. On 28 May 2008, Nepal was declared a republic. Despite his growing age and failing health, people reposed their faith in Koirala and he was elected the prime minister for the fifth time when he was eighty-two years old.

CONTRIBUTION

Koirala's greatest contribution was the restoration of democracy in the country. He not only established dialogue with Maoists but also convinced them to participate in nation-building. Amidst this, he also paid close attention to economic progress and the alleviation of poverty. A kind and compassionate stateman, Koirala would hear and incorporate others' advice.

He initiated the integration of Nepal's economy with the world's. Koirala breathed his last on 20 March 2010.

DID YOU KNOW?

- Koirala underwent a hunger strike for more than two weeks during his imprisonment in 1967.
- The Nepali government had forwarded the name of Koirala for the Nobel Peace Prize.
- His funeral was held in the famous Pashupatinath Temple in Kathmandu.

GOLDA MEIR

Golda Meir, the fourth, and the first woman prime minister of Israel, was an exemplary leader. She was a multifaceted woman—argumentative, charismatic, sympathetic, yet rigid and inflexible.

EARLY LIFE

Golda Meir was born on 3 May 1898 in Kiev, Russia. Her family moved to the US when she was eight years old, to escape the barbaric massacre of the Jews that had ripped through the Russian empire. They moved to Milwaukee where there were a number of Jewish families. Life was not easy there as well.

Growing up in a house full of many people, she learnt the value of patience. When ambitious Golda's parents prevented her from joining high school, the fifteen-year-old ran away from home and stayed with her sister at Denver. Golda became a Zionist there and believed in establishing a land for Jews in Palestine. Marriage to Morris Meyerson opened up a world of literature, music and art, a world denied to her before marriage.

LIFE IN PALESTINE

After marriage, Golda settled in Palestine. The couple lived in Merhavia Kibbutz which was a communal settlement. Life was tough but Golda did not mind doing physical labour, be it picking almonds or cooking food for her comrades. When her husband contracted malaria, Golda moved to Jerusalem and took up a job in the Jewish Labour Union where she soon rose up the ranks.

ENTERING POLITICS

Golda was always a passionate Zionist. She represented trade unions and was soon the spokesperson of the Zionist movement that demanded a homeland for the Jewish people. Golda began organizing fund-raising events in the US for the establishment of Israel. By the 1930s, Golda became an important member of the inner circle of David Ben Gurion, who went on to become the first prime minister of Israel. Gurion saw Golda as one of his trusted lieutenants.

FORMATION OF ISRAEL
World War II saw the displacement of many Jewish people across Europe. By 1947, more than 40,000 refugees were detained in various camps of Britain. Golda Meir had a difficult time negotiating their release. Shortly after, the UN voted to divide Palestine into two states—an Arab-born and a Jewish one. Within six months, the Jewish state of Israel was created. Palestine did not support the division of their state, and declared war against Israel. Golda went to the US to raise funds from the Jewish Americans. This paid for the war, and Israel declared its independence on 14 May 1948.

PRIME MINISTER
Golda had served the nation in various posts since 1948. She became the prime minister of Israel in 1969. The new country was still trying to settle the immigrants. Golda strengthened the economy as well as the military. She also established peace and safeguarded the hard-earned freedom of Israel.

Meir took up housing projects for her countrymen. She also established relations with the US and got economic and military aid from them. Golda also initiated peace talks with the Arab nations. Golda Meir breathed her last on 8 December 1978. She is remembered for her selfless service towards her nation and the personal sacrifices she had made for the nation.

DID YOU KNOW?

- Golda collected $50 million in 1948 to fight the war against the Arabs.
- Golda Meir went disguised as an Arab woman to meet King Abdullah of Oman to request him to not go to war against the Jews.
- She was termed 'the only man in the cabinet'.

HAILE SELASSIE

Considered to be the pillar of modern Ethiopia and a God-gifted person, Haile Selassie transformed Ethiopia into the nation it is today. Haile was the last claimant to the divine right of kings, that is, a legendary descendant of King Solomon and Queen Sheba.

EARLY LIFE
Haile Selassie was born on 23 July 1892 in a small thatched hut in Ejersa Gora. His childhood was as carefree as any other child and nobody expected that he would grow up into such a legend. For the outside world, Ethiopia was the land of King Solomon's mines and was securely hidden by giant mountains.

LEADER WITH FAR-SIGHTEDNESS
Emperor Menelik II, who was the cousin of Haile's father, did not have a male heir. Thus, Haile became the king in 1928. The younger population of his country looked up to him as their liberator Haile travelled to Europe to establish relations with the world.

He paid particular attention to education and policing. When Haile started his rule, Ethiopia had no buildings except the biggest building was a church or even roads. Haile took upon himself to build a palace—something that not only the Ethiopians but also the outsiders could appreciate. This palace is now a part of a museum.

IMPORTANT MEASURES TAKEN
Haile prioritized education and set up schools across Ethiopia and visited them regularly. However, Haile's decision to make education available to everyone was met with opposition from the nobility. The ordinary people too didn't want their children to go to schools as they felt that schools would contaminate their children. But Haile persisted, and even his servants' children were sent to school.

STRONG DIPLOMAT AND KING OF THE PEOPLE

Haile was a great diplomat. Haile was a staunch follower of tradition and struck a fine balance between the nobility and commoners. The church supported him in his drive for modernization and Haile was able to win the loyalty of around eighty-three ethnic tribes. By tradition, Haile was the head of the church, and therefore had the right to rule.

Instead of ruling comfortably from his palace, Haile travelled across his country to meet people. He sent young intelligent Ethiopians to Europe to come back with knowledge for the nation's development. Ethiopia was the first African country to join the League of Nations.

TRAGEDY

Tragedy struck in 1936 when Italy invaded Ethiopia. Haile was successful in getting help from the British. After reclaiming his kingship in 1941, he again started modernizing Ethiopia. He was, however, ousted from his dictatorial rule in 1974 by the opposition and kept under house arrest till his death in 1975.

DID YOU KNOW?

- Haile's palace was built in 1934 by 800 workers in eight months.
- He was the first monarch to have written a constitution for the governance of his country.
- It is believed that he was buried under one of the toilets in the palace. The king, however, got a regal funeral ceremony in 2000.

HAMID KARZAI

Hamid Karzai, former president of Afghanistan, rose as a great resistance to the formidable Taliban. He was a man who heralded a new beginning for Afghanistan after many years of suffering and bloodshed.

EARLY LIFE

Hamid Karzai was born on 24 December 1957, in Karz, Afghanistan, to a well-placed family. He is an ethnic Pasthun of the Popalzai tribe. Karzai received his early education from Afghanistan and came to India in an exchange programme and studied in Himachal University. Karzai is well-versed in several languages like Pashto, Persian, Hindi, French and English.

ENTERING POLITICS

When the Soviet Union attacked Afghanistan, Hamid moved to Pakistan to raise funds for supporting the anti-Soviet Mujahideen fighter's insurgency. He felt that his identity was under attack and he had to do something to save it. The Soviet pulled out of Afghanistan in 1989 and Karzai served as the deputy foreign minister in the Mujahideen transitional government. Karzai initially supported the political group, Taliban, believing they would check corruption and the unending conflicts between the Mujahideen warlords. When he broke away from them, his father was gunned down in 1999.

9/11 AND THEREAFTER

Hamid had started working closely with Ahmad Shah Massoud who was the military commander of the Northern Alliance, a group formed to fight the Taliban. After the attack on 9 September 2001 by the al-Qaeda, Karzai slipped into Kandahar to fight against the Taliban. The fall of Taliban made him a popular leader.

For the first time in history, the tribal chiefs of all the ethnic groups decided to settle their bitter rivalries and form an interim government. Karzai was selected as the interim president during the transition. However, in 2004 election, Karzai was elected as the president of the Islamic Republic of Afghanistan, winning twenty-one out of thirty-four provinces. A new constitution was formed which had a president directly elected by the people.

THE PRESIDENT AND HIS CHALLENGES

Karzai began by rebuilding institutions ravaged by many years of civil war and strife, but discovered that it was not easy forming negotiations with the people of other tribes. But not only did he learnt how to achieve this, he was also careful that the Taliban did not regain their power.

SECOND TERM AS THE PRESIDENT

The second presidential election, held in 2009, was followed by political turmoil which lasted for weeks. Karzai won the election again by a majority, against opponent Abdullah Abdullah, but critics say this election was fraudulent. Although Karzai had always enjoyed the support of the western allies initially, in his next term, he accused that US troops were unnecessarily causing Afghan civilian casualties. The fallout was such that Afghanistan refused to sign the agreement authorizing the US troops to stay in the country beyond their initial approval (of staying till 2014). Karzai's second term ended in September 2014. The former president still hopes for long-lasting peace for his country.

DID YOU KNOW?

- Karzai has survived at least four assassination attempts on his life.
- He has an honorary knighthood from Queen Elizabeth.
- He has honorary doctorates in literature and law from Boston University and Georgetown.

HELEN KELLER

Helen Keller is a source of inspiration to all the people of the world.

EARLY LIFE

Helen Keller was born on 27 June 1880 in Tuscumbia, US. She was a robust child who learnt to speak and walk quite early. However, stricken by illness at the age of two, she was left deaf, dumb and blind. It was devastating for the family. Bringing up Helen and providing her with education was a challenge for her mother. Helen had limited communication, and her only companion was Martha Washington, the daughter of the family cook. As she grew up, it got difficult to manage her, and her mother began to seek professional help.

TEACHER ANNE SULLIVAN

Michael Anaganos, the director of the Perkins Institute for the Blind in Boston, Massachusetts, recommended a young and bright teacher named Anne Sullivan. This was the beginning of a four-decade relationship.

Anne Sullivan's first task was to find a way to communicate with little Helen and win her trust. Sullivan tried to teach her words, but it was getting very difficult as Helen was not able to associate the words learnt with the right object. The breakthrough lesson came at the water pump when Helen learnt the word water and its spelling. It was as if a new world had opened for her, and Helen had learnt almost thirty words by the end of the day. After that day, there was no turning back.

BEGINNING FORMAL EDUCATION

Even though Anne Sullivan taught Helen all the subjects, the need of a formal education was still felt. Beginning her speech classes at the Horace Mann School for the Deaf at Boston, Helen would persevere for twenty-five long years to develop her speech. Helen had an insatiable thirst for learning and wanted to go to college and secure a degree. She wanted to disprove the fact that a disabled person did not have much to contribute to the society. She chose Radcliffe College because they did not want to give her admission. At Radcliffe she learnt French, German, Latin and Greek. Besides learning these languages, she mastered several methods of communication including touch-lip reading, Braille, typing and finger-spelling. She graduated in 1904 with a bachelor's degree in Arts.

MOUTHPIECE OF THE DISABLED

Helen's experiences at Radcliffe College had instilled in her a keen desire to battle for the equal status for the disabled. She also associated herself with a number of social issues like the fight for civil rights, and workers' rights.

Her heart went out for the cause of the deaf and the blind and she dedicated her life to it. As an ambassador for the American Foundation for the Blind, she worked resolutely to improve the opportunities available to them. Her constant persuasion resulted in the coming out of 'Talking Books' which enabled the blind people to listen to the recorded version of a book.

LEGACY

Time magazine has rightly named her as one of the 100 most influential people of the 20th century. Her passing away on 1 June 1968 was grieved by people across the world.

DID YOU KNOW?

- Helen loved animals, especially dogs, and owned a variety of them throughout her life.
- She travelled to thirty-nine countries to promote her ideas of equality and collaboration.
- She was the first woman to receive an honorary doctorate from Harvard.

HELMUT KOHL

Helmut Kohl, the last leader of West Germany and the first chancellor of unified Germany, was a man of fortitude who led the way to a modern Germany.

EARLY LIFE

Helmut Josef Michael Kohl was born on 3 April 1930, in Ludwigshafen am Rhein. He was the youngest of three children and his parents were conservative Catholics. World War II was a sad memory for Kohl as he recalled helping to search for the dead and injured in the rubble.

Kohl was a young teenager when he and his brother were taken in the Nazi Army. The family underwent massive trauma due to the death of his elder brother towards the end of the war. However, these were the experiences that made Kohl more resolute towards establishing peace in Europe.

ENTERING POLITICS

Politics and helping rebuild the German society went hand in hand for Kohl. He co-founded the Junge Union branch, the youth movement of the Christian Democrats (CDU), in Ludwigshafen. His political career began with his election to the regional parliament of Rhineland Palatinate in 1959. In the early part of the 1960s, he rapidly made progress in his political career and became the head of the parliamentary group. Kohl wanted reconciliation with France and the unification of Germany.

Kohl wanted to change Rheinland, the most backward state in West Germany, and attempted to do so when he was elected as the premier of Rheinland in 1969. Once he became a popular leader, his children could not meet him for long durations, making the family suffer. Eventually, Kohl moved from regional politics to national politics.

AS CHANCELLOR OF GERMANY

After entering national politics, Kohl expressed his desire to be the chancellor of Germany. The 1976 election was a decisive one as Kohl it, and became the leader of the Opposition. In 1983, Kohl fought the elections again and became the chancellor.

In 1984, Kohl met the French president, François Mitterrand, and signed a historic agreement of peace and friendly terms. He also went to the US with the same objective and met the then president, Ronald Reagan.

UNIFICATION OF GERMANY

The East Germans were eager to unify with West Germany but the West Germans were apprehensive. Kohl invited the East German leader Erich Honecker to visit West Germany. Meanwhile, Kohl had already established friendly terms with the US, which, in turn, appealed to the Soviet Union to pull down the Berlin Wall.

Kohl received verbal assurance from Mikhail Gorbachev, the general secretary of the Communist Party of the Soviet Union from 1985 to 1991, of non-interference and a peaceful reunification of Germany. Finally Kohl drew up a road map towards the cause of reunification, and the people in East Germany, who were reeling under poverty, saw Kohl as their saviour. Finally, in 1990, Germany was reunited and Helmut Kohl became the first chancellor of unified Germany. He died on 16 June 2017 of natural causes.

DID YOU KNOW?

- Helmut Kohl was a mentor and guide to Angela Markel.
- He loved his hometown Ludwigshafen and a dish from that place called 'saumagen', which means pig's stomach.
- He maintained a black diary which had strategic information about certain individuals.

HILLARY CLINTON

Hillary Clinton is a role model for women not only in her own country but across the globe. She remains an iconic female politician of the US.

EARLY LIFE

Hillary Clinton was born on 26 October 1947, in Illinois, Chicago. She was born into a modest family. Her father was a fabric store owner and her mother worked as a house maid when young. Thus, Hillary grew up respecting the dignity of hard work. She showed interest in politics at a very young age and was a staunch republican like her father. The speech of Reverend Martin Luther King Jr was a turning point in her life. She was drawn towards public service and changed from a republican to a democrat. After graduating from Wellesley College, where she was active in student politics, she went to Yale Law School.

CAREER

As a young lawyer, Hillary worked for the Children's Defense Fund and was also present during the then US president Richard Nixon's impeachment hearings. She then left Washington and went to Arkansas and became a faculty member in the Arkansas Law School. Meanwhile, she got married to Bill Clinton and joined the Rose Law Firm as a lawyer. She soon became their partner.

Hillary associated with issues of women, children and healthcare for all, and income equality between genders. As the head of the Arkansas Education Standard Committee, an appointment given by her husband, she contributed to reform the public schools of Arkansas.

FIRST LADY OF AMERICA

During the presidential campaign of her husband, Bill Clinton, Hillary emerged as a powerful partner. The president gave her a major responsibility of steering the task force on National Health Reform, and she soon emerged as a role model to Americans because of her dynamic nature.

During Bill Clinton's second term as the president, Hillary successfully worked for a bill to provide health insurance for children who were not covered under it.

MEMBER OF SENATE

After supporting her husband's political aspirations for almost three decades, in February 2000 she participated in the election of the senator of New York and became the first First Lady to be elected to public office. As senator, Hillary worked on the famous Senate Arms Services Committee and extended healthcare to National Guard members and their families.

PRESIDENTIAL RUN

In 2007, Hillary ran for the presidential elections but was defeated by Barack Obama. Eventually, Obama appointed Hillary as the secretary of state and gained respect of both foreign allies and adversaries for her work. In 2015, Hillary ran for the presidential elections again but lost to Donald Trump.

DID YOU KNOW?

- Hillary won the grammy for Best Spoken World Album for the audio recording of her book *It Takes a Village*.
- Hillary is the only former First Lady of the US who became a member of the US cabinet.
- Hillary rejected Bill's marriage proposals for two years before finally agreeing to marry him.

HO CHI MINH

Ho Chi Minh might have been small in size but he had the confidence of the mighty Himalayas.

EARLY LIFE

Ho Chi Minh was born on 19 May 1890 in Nghe An, a province in Vietnam. Having lost his mother when he was eleven, Ho had to take care of his younger siblings, as his father served as a local official and was mostly away. Ho studied Chinese and Confucianism. He also received French education in his teens. Vietnam was a French colony and Ho's father was aghast to see how easily the Vietnamese were relinquishing their rights to the French government.

Ho's father was dismissed from the bureaucracy and he spent the rest of his life trying to make a living. Ho inherited his father's rebelliousness as well as his wanderlust. At the age of twenty-one, he entered a merchant marine school where he learned how to be a kitchen helper. With this new skill, he travelled to Europe, Africa and even the US. In 1911, he was hired by a French ship and there he saw the terrible influence of colonialism.

BIRTH OF A REVOLUTIONARY

While in England, Ho worked under a chef and met many nationals from India, Ireland and Africa. This rekindled his spirit of nationalism and he decided to dedicate his life to the cause of his nation. He decided to go to Paris to learn how to become a revolutionary. He strived to organize the Vietnamese staying there since the end of the first World War into a movement to improve the conditions of his homeland. Frenchmen who were sympathetic to their cause encouraged him to join their socialist group and publish his own ideas. Soon, he, along with other Vietnamese, was not only publishing their own leaflets but were also smuggling them to Vietnam. Initially, he didn't want a revolution but better treatment of his people and equal rights. However, he was accused of treason and condemned to death if he ever returned to Vietnam. In 1920, he became one of the founding members of the French Communist Party. He was inspired by the ideology of Lenin and thus realized that liberty could not be achieved without a revolution.

RETURN HOME

Ho always believed that the right time would come when he would go back to his homeland and begin its liberation. He returned to Vietnam in 1941 after 30 years. He organized a guerrilla movement to drive the imperialists from his country. Since the majority of his countrymen were not familiar with him or his ideas, he simply talked to his people as a member of their family. Soon, many people joined him. Ho believed that getting American help was essential for the liberation of Vietnam, and after the US ended their war with Japan, he was able to procure weapons from them. He formed the Viet Minh (a league for Vietnamese Independence) to demand complete independence.

PRESIDENT OF VIETNAM

The Viet Minh attempted to seize power in 1945. The French did not want to give up their power so easily and war continued till 1954 when the French were forced to give up completely. The Vietnam War was fought between 1954 and 1959, a war that took a heavy toll on the people.

LATER YEARS

Ho remained the president after 1954 but gradually he started to transfer responsibilities to others. He was more active internationally to promote Vietnamese interests across the world. His health was failing and he breathed his last on 3 September 1969. Six years later, Vietnam was unified again.

DID YOU KNOW?

- He adopted the name Ho Chi Minh in 1941. It means 'Bringer of Light'.
- He helped the American forces in World War II to thwart the advances of Japan.
- Ho disappeared from the world stage for ten years and was once even reported dead.

HUGO CHÁVEZ

Hugo Chávez, the 45th president of Venezuela, was a man of the people. His uncompromising nature has given Venezuela a new lease of life.

CHILDHOOD
Born in Venezuela on 28 July 1954, Hugo's parents sent him to stay with his maternal grandmother, as there were no schools nearby. Although he grew up in poverty, he was a boy of vibrant energy and showed special interest in the study of history, and in sports, especially baseball.

JOINING THE MILITARY ACADEMY
At seventeen, Chávez joined the Venezuelan Military Academy. He graduated in 1975 and learnt not only about military tactics but also about various other topics. Chávez became the second lieutenant in the army and successfully suppressed rebel groups like the Red Flag Party which was a Marxist group led by poor peasants. But Chávez was gradually growing disillusioned with corruption and the unfair distribution of wealth in the country.

Chávez soon started to teach in the military academy, and by 1982, he had formed the group known as Revolutionary Bolivarian Movement-200, influenced by the South American revolutionary, Simón Bolívar. The number 200 conveyed the commemoration of the 200th birth anniversary of Bolívar. Chávez also influenced many students to join the group. Meanwhile, there were many cases of social unrest in the country as President Carlos Andrés Pérez caused dissent by his policies.

COUP D'ETAT
Although Chávez and his followers failed to overthrow the

government, they were successful in instilling hope for a changed government. Chávez was imprisoned for his act of defiance but after release in 1994, he spread his ideas of a revolution similar to Bolívar throughout Latin America. There was discontentment across the country due to economic disparity. Chávez decided to run the presidential elections to bring the desired changes. He formed the political party Movement for the Fifth Republic (MVR).

PRESIDENCY

Chávez was declared as the president of Venezuela on 2 February 1999. He took over the task of launching the Plan Bolívar 2000 for social welfare. Chávez's first priority was to work for the poor. He appointed officials for the execution of his plans. Chávez's own radio station and television channel made him popular. Chávez wanted to be transparent about his planning and execution.

He understood that some major changes had to be made at the basic level. Therefore, a new constitution was framed. Emphasis was laid on protection of the rights of the poor. The military was put in charge of national safety and was expected to aid national development and the maintenance of law and order in the society. Chávez also changed the name of his country to Bolivarian Republic Of Venezuela.

Chávez was elected for a second term in 2000. By then, he had formed friendly relations with the Cuban president, Fidel Castro. Chávez broke his ties with the US and even stopped the supply of oil under the influence of Castro.

Chávez was elected for the third term in 2006 and he lead to the propagation of democratic socialist ideals. He brought many enterprises under the government's control. Chávez combined the people of different parties under the single party of the United Socialist Party of Venezuela.

He passed away on 5 March 2013 due to cancer.

DID YOU KNOW?

- Besides baseball, Chávez also loved painting, writing fiction, drama and poetry.
- Chávez developed interest in communism after reading Che Guevara's memoir, *The Diary of Che Guevera*.
- Chávez came up with his own ideology which later came to be known as 'Chavism', which means an amalgamation of the different ideas, ideologies and government style of Chávez.

INDIRA GANDHI

Indira Gandhi was someone who faced umpteen challenges and roadblocks in her journey to success. Yet, Indira Gandhi, the first woman prime minister of India, the 'Iron Lady', has left behind a legacy for future generations.

EARLY LIFE
Indira Gandhi was born on 19 November 1917. She was the daughter of the first prime minister of India, Pt Jawaharlal Nehru, who named her Priyadarshani. Her grandfather Motilal Nehru named her Indira. Thus, Indira came to be known as Indira Priyadarshani Nehru. Indira grew up in a political atmosphere. Despite the fact that she was the only child and had so many people around her, she was often stressed in her childhood because her father used to be imprisoned frequently and her mother was ailing.

In 1936, tragedy struck Indira when her mother passed away. After completing her studies from Shantiniketan, she went to Summerville College in Oxford to pursue her studies. The father-daughter duo used to communicate through letters. She returned in 1941.

ENTERING POLITICS
In 1942, Indira married Feroze Gandhi, a prominent freedom fighter who had been imprisoned many times. He left his studies at the London School of Economics and joined the freedom movement. Indira and Feroze had two sons—Rajiv Gandhi and Sanjay Gandhi. Indira was well-versed with the political condition of India. India got her independence on 15 August 1947 and Jawaharlal Nehru became the first prime minister. Indira finally decided to enter politics and fought the 1959 parliamentary elections, which she won.

Tragedy struck Indira when Feroze Gandhi passed away at a

young age of 48. The death of Jawaharlal Nehru on 27 May 1964 was another devastating point in her life. Around this time, Indira was sworn in as the information and broadcasting minister in Lal Bahadur Shastri's cabinet.

AS PRIME MINISTER

Lal Bahadur Shastri died on 11 January 1966 and on 24 January Indira Gandhi was sworn in as the first female prime minister of India. Initially, Indira met with a lot of criticism but won the elections in 1967. In 1969, Indira nationalized fourteen major banks. She also abolished the Privy Purse, which ensured monetary benefits to the former rulers of the princely states. Indira brought an agricultural revolution in the country which resulted in greater crop production, and soon India turned from an importer to an exporter of food grains. The elections in 1971 saw Indira as a more resolute woman. Her slogan 'Garibi Hatao' received a lot of support and she emerged victorious, winning 352 parliamentary seats. That year was also decisive because she won a major victory in a war with Pakistan and was instrumental in the independence of Bangladesh. She also extended a friendly hand to the Soviet Union to counter the US.

INDIRA'S ASSASSINATION

With reports of instability in the government, Indira imposed a state of Emergency in 1975. Indira lost elections in 1977 but in the 1980 general elections, she emerged victorious and was sworn in as the prime minister.

The accidental death of her son Sanjay Gandhi left her desolate. Rajiv Gandhi had just started shouldering the responsibilities of the party when the country was shocked by Indira Gandhi's assassination on 31 October 1984. She was killed by her bodyguards as a reaction to Operation Blue Star which allowed the Indian Army to enter the premises of the Golden Temple to nab terrorists.

DID YOU KNOW?

- Indira joined the league of independence struggle at the early age of five when she burnt her doll because it was made in England.
- The two 'Iron Ladies', Indira Gandhi and Margaret Thatcher, were very good friends.
- She led the country into the nuclear age with its first underground detonation in 1974.

JAWAHARLAL NEHRU

Jawaharlal Nehru was the leader who ushered in the independence of India as its first prime minister. His exemplary contribution set the pace for the country to become a leading democracy in the world.

EARLY LIFE

Jawaharlal Nehru was born on 14 November 1889 to a prominent lawyer Motilal Nehru and Swaroop Rani. He was the eldest of three children. Nehru received his early education at home and later went to Harrow, a school in England. He graduated from Trinity College and got a degree in law from the City Law School, London. Nehru showed signs of a nationalist since childhood and was also interested in the culture of India.

BACK HOME

Although he joined the Allahabad High Court under his lawyer father after he returned to India in 1912, he soon decided to join the Congress to do more socially engaging work. In 1916, he got married to Kamala Kaul.

ENTRY INTO POLITICS

During his stay abroad, he was influenced by the western concepts of freedom and socialism and wanted to see them materialize in India. Jawaharlal joined the Home Rule League started by Lokmanya Tilak and Annie Besant. In 1916, Nehru met Gandhiji in the Lucknow Congress and was impressed by his 'unpolitical' stance. Gandhiji's formation of the Satyagraha Society to disobey the British rule and the Jallianwallah Bagh massacre jolted Nehru and he became active in politics.

Nehru gave up his practice of law and was elected the vice president of the Allahabad District Congress Committee in 1920. He toured the interiors of Uttar Pradesh and got insight of the abject condition of farmers. Thereafter, Nehru, along with Gandhiji, began working for the agrarian cause of India.

STRIDING TOWARDS FREEDOM

After plunging into politics, Nehru toured India at a frantic pace, meeting people and getting to discover the real India. In 1927, in the Madras Congress, Nehru gave concrete shape to the vision of complete independence for India. Nehru mobilized people and gave a clarion call for 'Swaraj'. In 1929, Nehru was elected the president of the All India Congress. The unfurling of India's flag the same year on the banks of the river Ravi created a nationwide stir and brought Nehru to the forefront. Eventually, Nehru was imprisoned for nine years. In prison, he spent his time reading and writing, and authored two books—*Discovery of India* and *The Unity of India*.

WORLD WAR II AND THE QUIT INDIA MOVEMENT

When World War II started, Viceroy Linlithgow unilaterally declared India on the side of Britain, without consulting elected Indian representatives. This infuriated the Congress and Nehru who informed the imperial government that they would co-operate only under certain conditions—Britain must give an assurance of full independence to India after the war, allow elections for a Constituent Assembly to frame the new constitution, and Indians must be immediately included in the central government.

When all these demands were denied, Nehru and Gandhi declared civil disobedience in 1940. The government tried to pacify them but to no avail. The entire Congress working committee, including Gandhi and Nehru, were arrested and imprisoned. Nehru was released in 1945 when Lord Wavell wanted to break the deadlock. Nehru played a key role in these negotiations and proved his statesmanship. Finally, on 15 August 1947, India became independent.

THE FIRST PRIME MINISTER OF INDEPENDENT INDIA

Being a statesman, he laid down the foundation for the new India. Nehru laid great emphasis on science and technology, and established a chain of laboratories for scientific research. He also set up the planning commission in 1950 and paid attention to the development of the tribals. Nehru's patronage for Indian art, culture and literature is also noteworthy.

Nehru's remarkable life came to an end on 27 May 1964.

DID YOU KNOW?

- The Nehru jacket is named after him which he began wearing after he shunned western clothing.
- He was nominated for the Nobel Peace Prize eleven times.
- There were four known assassination attempts on Nehru.

JOAN OF ARC

Joan of Arc is celebrated for her bravery and patriotism all over the world. She was an illustrious military leader acting under divine guidance, and was hailed as the symbol of French patriotism.

EARLY LIFE

Joan of Arc was born in 1412 to a poor tenant farmer in Domremy, France. She was a happy and pious girl who loved working in her father's farm. When others were sick, she would visit them to help them feel better.

France was going through a tumultuous time and was embroiled in the Hundred Years' War with England. France was faring badly in the war. Joan started to have mystical visions, urging her to lead a pious life, which, over time, became very vivid. She saw herself designated as the saviour of France and decided to go to the king of France and speak of her belief that France would be free. The king allowed her go to battle against the norm.

BATTLE PREPARATIONS

Although King Charles was apprehensive about her claims, he allowed her to march to Orleans with the French Army in order to win back parts of northern France which was under seige by the English king Henry VI. Joan was only seventeen at that time; she cut her hair short and dressed like a man. Joan's strategies galvanized the army into launching successful attacks. The English could not withstand the attack, and Orleans was liberated. On 18 July 1429, King Charles was crowned as Charles VII, during which she occupied an important place in the ceremonies.

CAPTURE AND TRIAL

During an attack with the Burgundians to win back Compiègne,

Joan was taken captive. The Burgundians sold her off to the English for 10,000 francs. The English were interested in eliminating Joan because they wanted to prove to the world that Charles VII owed his coronation to a heretic. Charles VII did not do anything to release her and Joan was turned over to the church with an appeal that she should be tried for heresy.

Joan's trial was held by Bishop Pierre Cauchon who was a supporter of the English. The church tried many ways to make her plead guilty, but was not successful. She was tried for sorcery, but when that failed, they charged her for wearing men's clothes, which was heretical in the 15th century.

DEATH

The tribunal announced that they had found Joan guilty of heresy and magic. On the fateful day of 30 May 1431, she was taken to the marketplace of Rouen by an escort of 800 armed Frenchmen, where she was burnt alive at the stake. Later, her ashes were gathered and scattered in the Seine.

RETRIAL

Charles VII ordered an investigation into Joan's death, and after seven years, the tribunal's verdict was declared to be null and void. Joan was declared innocent in 1456 and canonized as a saint in 1920. Joan is considered the patron saint of France today.

DID YOU KNOW?

- Joan of Arc was arrested with more than 70 charges, including horse theft and sorcery.
- She inspired the bob haircut which originated in Paris in 1909.
- Her voices guided her towards the church of St Catherine where they told her that she would find a sword; miraculously, it was there.

JOKO WIDODO

Joko Widodo, the president of Indonesia, is often referred to as the Indonesian rockstar politician. He believes in staying grounded even while hobnobbing with the elites.

EARLY LIFE

Joko Widodo was born into a poor family of carpenters on 21 June 1961 at Surakarta, Indonesia. Widodo grew up in the slums of Surakata and began working at a very early age. Despite various hurdles, he completed his education and earned a degree in forestry engineering from the Gadjah Mada University.

EARLY CAREER AND POLITICS

Although Widodo was a successful exporter of furniture, the affairs of his country pulled him towards politics and he became the mayor of Surakata. People soon found in him a leader who was honest, believed in reforms and understood their plight.

In 2012, Widodo became the governor and began to encourage small industries, public healthcare and education.

CHALLENGES AND ACHIEVEMENTS

In 2014, Widodo was elected the president, but he faced a lot of criticism over human rights issues and the slow economic growth of the country. Since fishing was an important source of livelihood in Indonesia, Widodo took firm steps to stop vessels indulging in illegal fishing.

Drug addiction was another major challenge in the country. Widodo showed no mercy towards drug peddlers and did not hesitate to issue the death penalty to those involved in the crime.

After being elected as the president, Widodo travelled extensively across the country and tried to assuage the difficulties faced by the people. He went around giving assurance to Indonesians about his willingness to speed up building the infrastructure of the country.

He has begun progressive programmes like issuing Smart Jakarta Cards and Healthy Jakarta Card to benefit the poor. Besides, he is trying to end corruption and seek foreign investment.

Widodo appreciates the importance of oceans for Indonesia and is keen on preserving the marine health of the nation. He has set the right track for growth of the country.

DID YOU KNOW?

- While contesting the elections, Widodo raised funds by selling red plaid shirts, his favourite, instead of seeking political favours.
- He often dresses in plain clothes and appears in markets to gauge the life of the people. This is called 'blusukan', and he loves it.
- He is a big fan of heavy metal music. Some of his favourites are Metallica and Megadeth.

JOMO KENYATTA

A charismatic man and a great orator, Jomo Kenyatta was a powerful leader who shaped the history of Kenya.

EARLY LIFE

Kenyatta had a very humble beginning. He was born around 1894 in a family of farmers who bred sheep and goats. He lost his parents in his early childhood and was brought up by his grandfather. Since Kenya was under British imperialism, Kenyatta was denied admission to a school. A resolute boy, he earned his way to school by working for a white man. However, the discrimination left him enraged.

PIOLITICAL ACTIVISM AND IMPRISONMENT

During World War I, when the British started employing Kenyan men into the British Army, Kenyatta refused to fight for the white people and joined the East Africa Association (EAA), a movement against the government. When the EAA was disbanded in 1925, its members reformed as the Kikuyu Central Association, with the sole aim of ousting the British from their soil. Kenyatta became the secretary general three years later. Meanwhile, the British were thinking of merging Kenya, Uganda and Tanganyika. Kenyatta was completely against this and tried to make the British postpone their decision.

In London, he lobbied for his country and also to complete his education. On his return in 1946, he took up the leadership of the newly-formed Kenya African Union (KAU); he was elected the president of the union in June 1947.

The British declared a state of emergency in the light of violence by Mau Mau activists, and many Kenyans, including 60-year-old Kenyatta were arrested in 1952 on the charge of heading the group even though he denied such involvement. He was imprisoned for seven years, but after his release, he became even more popular.

KENYA'S INDEPENDENCE

Kenya was declared independent on 12 December 1963 and Kenyatta became the prime minister. The numerous European settlers in Kenya were scared of what would happen to them. However, he allowed them to stay in Kenya. Tolerance, generosity and cooperation were the pillars of the new Kenya. In 1964, when Kenya became a one-party republic as the main opposition party went into voluntary liquidation, Kenyatta became the first president of Kenya under a new constitutional amendment.

NATION-BUILDING

The task of nation-building fell on Kenyatta. He paid particular attention to infrastructure and the growth of the economy. He set up relations with other countries and visited many head dignitaries across the world and secured foreign funds. In 1966, he set up the Jomo Kenyatta Foundation which focused on providing education to deprived students. He also improved the health and sanitation of the country. The farmers were given loans and better quality seeds to increase yield. He also ensured that the people of Kenya would be unified despite the presence of different ethnic groups.

LEGACY

A charmer when it came to talking to people, Kenyatta was also called the Founding Father of Kenya. His demise on 22 August 1978 was mourned by the entire nation. All the Kenyan currencies bear his face.

DID YOU KNOW?

- Kenyatta enacted the role of a tribal chief in the movie *Sanders of the River*.
- He always carried a fly-whisk with him, which symbolized his power.
- He was lovingly addressed as Mzee.

JOSIP BROZ TITO

Josip Broz Tito, the president of Yugoslavia from 1953 to 1980, was a man who had the courage to stand alone and steer his country towards development.

EARLY LIFE

Josip Broz was born in a poor peasant's house in 1892, in Kumrovec, a small village in the northern Croatian region. He soon started to work, and witnessed many hardships in life. The death of his six siblings taught Tito the important lesson of how fragile and precious life is. At the young age of eighteen, Tito went to eastern Europe and spent time observing people.

Tito was inducted into the Austro-Hungarian Army when World War I erupted. He proved his military and leadership skills in the war and was made the sergeant major at the young age of twenty-one. Tito was taken prisoner in Russia and got his freedom just when the Russian Revolution started in 1917.

JOINING POLITICS

Tito returned to Croatia and found employment difficult. He joined the Communist Party even though it was banned, and participated actively in the Trade Union Movement. Being influenced by the Marxist-Leninist vision of the power of the working class, he began to question why he and his comrades should toil for the benefit of the monarchy.

In 1928, he was sentenced to five years' imprisonment for spreading propaganda. After his release, Tito was called upon by Moscow to act as an international communist spy. Thus, Tito became a master of disguise using many passports and different identities. It was in one such disguise that he assumed the name Tito, which stuck on.

ASSUMING POWER

In 1941, when Tito was the head of the communist Yugoslav Party, Germany invaded Yugoslavia and it destroyed the nation. However, Tito formed a group of freedom fighters to expel foreign invaders, and also strived to liberate his country from its old monarchy.

PRESIDENTIAL TERM

The Communist Party led by Tito emerged as the single party that could take over the reins of the country. He served as the prime minister from 1945 to 1953 and the country was named Federal People's Republic of Yugoslavia.

CONTRIBUTION

Coming to power, Tito started with the task of nation-building. He formed a federation of six nations. Tito refused to relinquish Yugoslavia's independence even when faced with threats from the powerful Russian leader, Joseph Stalin. Decentralizing the economy and establishing the system of worker self-management doubled the production and improved living conditions of the people. Tito established relations with western nations and was the first communist country to welcome foreign visitors.

Yugoslavia was one of the founding members of the non-aligned movement, which helped Tito develop strong ties with the third world countries. Tito ensured freedom of speech and religious freedom for his people. Tito breathed his last on 4 May 1980.

DID YOU KNOW?

- Tito did not receive formal education beyond his primary school.
- When presented at the court after his arrest in 1928, he shouted to a packed courtroom, 'Long live the Communist party. Long live the revolution.
- Hitler offered a reward of 100,000 Reichsmark to anyone who would capture or assassinate Tito.

JUSTIN TRUDEAU

Justin Trudeau, the prime minister of Canada, is a man of the people, the 'rockstar politician'. His energy and unpretentiousness makes him a popular leader of this North American nation.

EARLY LIFE

Justin Trudeau was born on 25 December 1971 near Ottawa, Canada. His father, Pierre Trudeau, was the former prime minister of Canada. Trudeau received a very normal upbringing despite his father occupying such an important position in the country. He attended the same school as his father. In 1998, he earned a master's degree in environmental geography from the University of British Colombia.

ENTERING POLITICS

Trudeau had never shown any interest in politics before the death of his father. In 2008, when he delivered a moving eulogy at his father's funeral, he was seen as a person with the potential to be a statesman. But Trudeau did not want to enter politics then, and instead became the chairman of the board of Katimavik, a youth service initiative started by his father. However, he could not avoid the political arena for long.

In 2007, Trudeau began his campaign for a parliament seat representing Montreal. In 2013, he was the Liberal Party's leader. After two years, Trudeau sought to contest for the highest political position in the country—the prime minister. His campaign included promises to boost the economy and fight unemployment.

He finally led his party to success and was sworn into office on 4 November 2015.

CONTRIBUTION

When in office, Trudeau announced infrastructure development worth $180 billion to be spent in ten years. The plan focused on public transport, infrastructure in rural areas and affordable housing for people.

Trudeau believes in providing religious freedom to people. He also proclaimed that his government would uphold women's rights and remove gender inequality in all sectors. Trudeau made several reforms, including the complete overhaul of the appointment process of the senate. The criteria for appointment to senate now include integrity of character, community service, required experience and leadership qualities. He also addressed the rights of Canada's indigenous people. Trudeau also came up with a new ballot system which gives the voters the option to rank the candidates in order of preference. Trudeau's concern for the environment also makes him a leading global statesman.

FOREIGN RELATIONS

Under Trudeau's leadership, the Canadian government decided to welcome around one million immigrants over a period of three years. This decision has created good relations with the rest of the world. Trudeau has also accepted many refugees to the country. He eased regulations pertaining to foreign travel. No wonder that as the prime minister, Trudeau's popularity remains on the rise.

DID YOU KNOW?

- American president Richard Nixon predicted just a few months after Trudeau's birth that he would become the prime minister of Canada one day.
- Trudeau has performed various odd jobs during his life such as being a bouncer in a nightclub, a rafting instructor, a mathematics teacher, a radio host, etc.
- Half of the cabinet positions were given to women, as Trudeau wanted gender parity in the government.

K.M. CARIAPPA

Kodandera Madappa Cariappa is certainly one of the most distinguished soldiers of India. His unrelenting patriotism has left a strong legacy for all Indians to be proud of.

EARLY LIFE
Born in the Coorg district of Karnataka on 28 January 1899, his father worked in the Revenue Department of the British government. He grew up listening to the fascinating stories of soldiers and their heroic deeds in World War I. After Cariappa learnt that Indians were being recruited into the army as officers, he immediately applied to the new cadet college being set up in Indore and rose to become the best cadet in the batch.

CAREER
Cariappa was chosen to be sent for further training to the renowned Royal Military College in Sandhurst. After being made the second lieutenant in 1919, he was posted first to Carnatic Infantry and later to Rajput Light Infantry, which went on to become his permanent regimental home. He proved his mettle and was the first Indian to be given the command of an army unit.

Cariappa won wide acclaim for the manner in which he dealt with the case of the Indian National Army's (INA) prisoners. In fact, he was responsible for the release of most of the INA officers. As the country was making preparations for its independence, Cariappa was the first Indian chosen to undergo a training course at the Imperial Defence College, Camberley, UK.

COMMANDER-IN-CHIEF
Cariappa was chosen as the commander-in-chief of the Western Command. Therefore, the security of sensitive areas like Kashmir

and the Leh-Ladakh region fell upon him. Under his able leadership, the Lashkars of Pakistan were pushed back, and places like Poonch, Drass and Kargil were recaptured. An important connection was also established with Leh.

Cariappa took over as the commander-in-chief of the Indian Army on 15 January 1949. He was responsible for the formation of the Brigade of Guards where troops from all parts of India serve together—the Parachute Regiment, an airborne infantry, and also the Territorial Army, which initiated the inclusion of willing civilians as a second line of defence after the regular Indian Army.

IDENTITY BUILDING OF INDIAN ARMY

K.M. Cariappa took upon himself the great task of building an identity of the Indian Army. He began by ensuring that the army remains an autonomous body and is not under the influence of politics.

Cariappa had remarkable farsightedness and therefore reservations based on caste or tribe was turned down by him; serving in the army is possible only through merit.

LEGACY

Cariappa retired from the Army on 14 January 1953 after his illustrious career of three decades. He was conferred with the rank of field marshal as a tribute to his commendable service. Till his last breath, he was a soldier, and often went to meet other soldiers to boost their morale. He breathed his last on 15 May 1993.

DID YOU KNOW?

- Cariappa was honoured with the Order of the British Empire in June 1945 for his excellent service in Burma wherein he pushed back the Japanese.
- There is a park in Baramulla in honour of Cariappa as he had provided food to the hungry villagers in 1947 during the war in Kashmir.

KAILASH SATYARTHI

Kailash Satyarthi is an inspiration to many. He is an angel to the children he saved.

EARLY LIFE

Kailash Sharma was born in Vidisha, Madhya Pradesh on 11 January 1954. His father was a police officer. He was a compassionate child who felt gravely for the underprivileged people. The plight of deprived children moved him so much that as a young boy he formed a football club to raise money for the payment of school fees for poor children and ate the food prepared by untouchables and changed his surname to Satyarthi to protest caste distinctions.

EARLY CAREER

Even though Satyarthi received many lucrative offers thanks to his engineering degree, he quit his job in 1980 and decided to dedicate his life towards the emancipation of underprivileged children.

Satyarthi started the magazine, *Sangharsh Jaari Rahega*—which highlighted the pathetic life of vulnerable people. He started working under the tutelage of Swami Agnivesh for the cause of women and children. However, he soon broke away from him as he did not want to have any collaboration with activism related to religion.

Bachpan Bachao Andolan (BBA), the non-profit organization, founded by Satyarthi aims to free children from the bondage of child labour. Often, when brick and carpet factories were targeted by the organization, Satyarthi and his comrades were beaten up and there were some attempts of assassination as well. His family members were also attacked several times but Sathyarthi never gave up.

He also launched a programme, Bal Mitra Gram, that promoted child-friendly villages which ensured the right to education to all children.

REACHING OUT INTERNATIONALLY

He collaborated with foreign NGOs also working for the cause of children. This led to the formation of South Asian Coalition on Child Servitude (SACCS), which partnered with organizations of Bangladesh, Pakistan, Sri Lanka and Nepal to eradicate child labour.

In 1989, Satyarthi initiated a protest march against the exploitation of children, called the Global March against Child Labour, in which around a hundred countries participated. He travelled almost 80,000 km to draw international attention to the grave problem of child labour in India and other developing and under-developed countries. His demands led to the ratification by the International Labour Organization for setting the standard for unacceptable forms of child labour, minimum age of employment and requirements for hazardous work.

Satyarthi was also the co-founder of the global campaign for education, which defended education as a universal human right. In 2001, he became a founding member of the UNESCO group that looks into education for all. In 2017, Sathyarthi began a march across twenty-four states in thirty-five days as a protest against child sexual abuse and child trafficking. He and his family received many life threats, but he also managed to gather extensive support from Indians across the nation.

Satyarthi was awarded with the Nobel Peace Prize in 2014 for his work.

DID YOU KNOW?

- Satyarthi is a great cook and loves to cook in his free time.
- He dedicated his Nobel Peace Prize to the nation. The 18-carat gold medal is in the Rashtrapati Bhavan.
- His organization BBA has freed around 80,000 children across India from the grips of child labour.

KENNETH DAVID KAUNDA

Kenneth David Kuanda, the first president of Zambia, is an effective statesman and politician. Many feel that there can be no Zambia without him.

EARLY LIFE

Kenneth David Kaunda was born on 28 April 1924 at Lubwa Mission in Chinsali, Northern Rhodesia (modern Zambia). His father was a minister in the church and his mother was the first African woman to teach in colonial Zambia. Kaunda received his early education in Zambia and became a teacher in colonial Zambia, and later, in Tanzania.

RISE AGAINST COLONIAL RULE

Kaunda returned to Zambia in 1949 with the dream of liberating his country from the colonial rule. He became an interpreter and advisor to a white settler who was a member of the Legislative Council. This gave Kaunda an insight into the workings of the colonial government. Kaunda soon joined the first anti-colonial organization, African National Congress, and became its secretary general. Soon, Kaunda broke away and created the Zambian African National Congress aimed at 'positive non-violent action' against the government.

Kaunda was imprisoned for going against the government and he earned the status of a national hero. He was released in 1960 and in early 1961, the British announced the formal decolonization of Zambia, leading to its independence on 24 October 1964.

PRESIDENT OF INDEPENDENT ZAMBIA

The first general elections in Zambia were held in 1962. The United National Independence Party, headed by Kaunda, won majority seats.

Kaunda was unanimously chosen as the first president of free Zambia and he was successful in avoiding a civil war in the country. To avoid inter-party political violence, Kaunda imposed one party rule in Zambia. Kaunda believed that no African had a right to feel free until every inch of Africa was not free. Kaunda served as the president from 1964 to 1991.

A CHARISMATIC LEADER
Kaunda has always been close to people. Kaunda was so popular amongst his people that people rushed to meet him whenever he came out of his house. Despite facing atrocities from the colonial government and being imprisoned several times, he came out with no bitter feelings for anyone. His cry of 'One Zambia, one Nation' is still remembered in the country.

Kaunda took many steps to improve the economy of Zambia. He set up many schools, colleges and universities. Kaunda also privatized many companies and opened doors to foreign investment.

POST PRESIDENCY
Kaunda is actively engaged with several organizations and continues to render his services. He has brought a behavioural change among the youth and educates them about issues like HIV/AIDS.

DID YOU KNOW?
- Due to his non-violent methods, Kuanda earned the title, 'Gandhi of Africa'.
- He is a strict vegetarian.
- He used to play soccer and now he enjoys playing golf.

KHAN ABDUL GHAFFAR KHAN

E ven though Khan Abdul Ghaffar Khan was a tall and frail Pathan, there was no frailty in his ideology. He was a progressive leader whose name stands out amidst violence and gunshots.

EARLY LIFE

Ghaffar Khan was born on 6 February 1890 to a farmer in Afghanistan, Behram Khan, who was the chief of a small tribe. His father valued education and decided to send his children to a school run by the British. He was selected to join the British Indian Army but soon dropped the idea because of the injustice meted out to the natives.

GHAFFAR KHAN AS A VISIONARY

Ghaffar Khan centred his entire struggle around his people in Afghanistan. He defied the British and the Russians as he wanted to achieve a free and democratic land for the Pathans. Ghaffar Khan was a visionary and realized quite early that the Pathans could find their liberation only through education. Thus, he opened schools which made the British feel threatened. Consequently, the British imprisoned and tortured him. But Ghaffar Khan became even more resolute.

GIRLS' EDUCATION

Ghaffar Khan encouraged girls' education, a rare act of courage in those days. He not only educated his daughters but also sent them abroad for higher studies. A champion of women's rights, he desired that they should come out of the 'purdah'. He also opened many schools for girls.

REBEL THROUGH WORDS

In 1924, Ghaffar Khan started a newspaper called *Pakhtun*, which was the first national newspaper to reach out to the masses, and gained immense popularity. He also travelled to India to collect funds for his cause. In 1928, he met Mahatma Gandhi and Jawaharlal Nehru and returned with a renewed fervour to arouse the nationalistic feeling he had witnessed in India.

KHUDAI KHIDMATGARS
In 1929, he formed the Khudai Khidmatgars, meaning the Servants of God. Anyone joining this organization had to take the vow of non-violence. They were targeted by the British who ordered their soldiers to fire at the unarmed Khidmadgars and beat up the Pathans. Despite such inhuman atrocities, the Pathans did not give up, and the Khidmatgars did not choose violence. Ghaffar Khan used to walk across villages meeting people, settling feuds and urging them not to resort to violence for settling their issues.

Ghaffar Khan believed that one could pray to God in any language he wanted. He read the Gita with equal devotion as he read the Quran and believed that service to humanity was the greatest religion. He said that a true Muslim was one who did not hurt others, either in action or in words.

PARALLEL WITH GANDHI
Khan was called Frontier Gandhi as there are many similarities between him and Gandhi. Both of them fought for the rights of the unprivileged, they stayed away from power, resisted oppression and tried to remove poverty. Their only weapons were courage and consciousness. Ghaffar Khan was against the partition of India and fought for India's independence. He was imprisoned for opposing partition. However, he fell critically ill and was released from prison.

ROLE AFTER PARTITION
Since Ghaffar Khan could not stop partition, he extended his support to the young nation, Pakistan. However, things did not go well between him and Muhammad Ali Jinnah. Thus, he formed Pakistan's first opposition party, the Pakistan Azad Party, in 1948 and pledged

to indulge in constructive opposition. But he was arrested several times between 1948 and 1956 for opposing government policies. Ghaffar Khan was arrested again in 1973 and he called Bhutto, the then prime minister, a dictator of the worst kind.

Ghaffar Khan's health started deteriorating, and he breathed his last on 20 January 1988.

DID YOU KNOW?

- Ghaffar Khan was bestowed the Bharat Ratna in 1987.
- He was put under house arrest by the Pakistan government without any reason from 1948 to 1954.
- Ghaffar Khan never held any position of importance in his life, yet was respected worldwide.

LEE KUAN YEW

L ee Kuan Yew was a visionary and thinker whose nation's integrity was his topmost priority. The first prime minister of Singapore, Yew devoted his life to the cause of nation-building.

EARLY LIFE

Lee Kuan Yew was born on 16 September 1923 to Lee Chin Koon and Chua Jim Neo in Singapore. He had a very simple upbringing as his parents had lost their fortune in the Great Depression. Lee Kuan was a bright student and was awarded scholarships at both school and college levels. He earned a law degree from Fitzwilliam College in England and returned to Singapore only to discover that he was more interested in politics.

ENTRY INTO POLITICS

Lee Kuan Yew was dismayed by the prevailing conditions of Singapore under the British rule. Singapore was ruled by a governor and a legislative council which usually comprised of wealthy Chinese businessman. The natives demanded constitutional reforms and independence.

Lee Kuan felt an urge to change the fate of his nation and started the People's Action Party (PAP) on 21 November 1954 together with some other young men. He became the secretary general and remained so till 1992. In 1955, he secured the Tanjong Pagar seat and became the opposition's leader. He represented PAP in London twice to discuss the constitutional needs of Singapore.

The tables turned in the 1959 elections when he won the majority votes and he was sworn in as the first prime minister of Singapore. He was an anti-colonialist and demanded massive social reform.

LEE KUAN AS THE PRIME MINISTER

Lee Kuan started with the construction of his nation. His main agenda was development. He focused on issues of urban development and housing, rights of women and education. In 1963, Singapore declared complete independence from British rule. The Republic of Singapore was born on 9 August 1965. The major problem for Singapore was that it did not have natural resources, and thus had to depend for everything on others. Moreover, Singapore did not have any national defence forces which were important for any independent country. Lee had to take some quick decisions to make his country self-reliant.

With unemployment at an all-time high, Lee Kuan and his economic team decided to have an export-oriented industrialization, and welcomed multinational companies. He worked relentlessly and ensured that Singapore was accepted in the UN and into the association of South East Asian Nations in the year of their independence. Compulsory military service was introduced in 1967, and English, Malay, Chinese and Tamil were accorded the status of national languages. He created the body called Corrupt Practices Investigation Bureau which was empowered to not only investigate bank accounts and income details of people under suspicion but also arrest if someone was found guilty.

LATER YEARS

Lee Kuan resigned in 1990 but continued to advise the government. He was a great statesman and helped transform Singapore from a third world country to a first-class nation. Lee Kuan passed away in 2015.

DID YOU KNOW?

- Lee Kuan loved fitness and therefore exercised on the treadmill thrice a day.
- He never wasted a single penny of the taxpayers' money on himself.

LEON TROTSKY

Leon Trotsky was the man behind the Russian revolution and the formation of the Red Army. He was a great revolutionary—uncompromising and courageous.

EARLY LIFE

Leon Trotsky was born as Lev Bronstein on 7 November 1879 in Yanovka, Ukraine, in the Russian empire. His parents were simple Jewish farmers. Trotsky started going to school when he was eight and was inspired by Marxism in his final years in high school.

BECOMING A REVOLUTIONARY AND THE RUSSIAN REVOLUTION

Trotsky embraced Marxism when Russia was entering into a difficult period of strikes and distress. He used to work late into the night writing leaflets expressing his agitation and distribute them to factory workers. Soon, Trotsky was arrested and sent to Siberia. He escaped to London, where he met his ideal, Vladimir Lenin.

The incident of Bloody Sunday—wherein hundreds of Russian protestors were gunned down for participating in a peaceful march on 9 January 1905—triggered the Russian Revolution. Trotsky played a significant role in this. He was barely twenty-six, but was chosen as the president of the revolution.

WORLD WAR I

After World War I, Trotsky condemned the war and joined the Russian Social Democrats, refusing to support the Czar's war effort regime. Trotsky published a daily newspaper from Paris in which he defended internationalism and opposed the imperialists' war. He was expelled from Paris after which he went to New York. Despite many atrocities and difficulties, the ordinary people were gradually turning against the war. Meanwhile, in 1917, the Czar was overthrown from the Soviet. A provincial government was formed, but Trotsky stood against it.

REVOLUTION OF 1917

Trotsky played a very significant role in the revolution of 1917 which saw the toppling of the provincial government led by Alexander Kerensky. The revolution would never have been successful without the likes of Trotsky and Lenin. His slogan was 'All power to the Soviets'. This led the Bolsheviks, a faction of the Marxist Russian Social Democratic Labour Party, to win the majority seats, as it inspired the common people to extend their support.

CIVIL WAR

When the civil war broke out in Russia in 1918, Trotsky organized the Red Army and led it to victory. Trotsky travelled across Russia in his famous armed train that contained not only ammunition, but also cinema, and books of propaganda.

ROLE IN GOVERNMENT

Trotsky was the foreign commissioner, and his task was to implement Bolshevik ideals across the country. Trotsky also entered peace negotiations with the neighbouring powers. Having successfully mitigated the civil war, Trotsky turned his attention to the economy of the country.

Trotsky wanted some flexibility and relaxation in the stringent laws of centralization. He felt that market forces should be allowed to operate, but he was opposed vehemently by the Bolshevik government. Trotsky also sought to use the army to help in the administration of the transportation system.

Trotsky was among the top five policymakers of the Communist Party. Being a pragmatic statesman, he wanted that the trade unions should only administer the working conditions of the factories instead of the whole industry.

DEATH

There was a struggle for succession after the death of Lenin. The obvious choice was, of course, Trotsky, but Joseph Stalin, a powerful leader, wanted all power for himself. Trotsky was expelled from the party and he, along with his principal followers, was exiled to a remote part of Russia. He had to keep on moving from one place to another. In August 1940, he was assassinated by a Spanish communist and a probable agent of Stalin.

DID YOU KNOW?

- Leon Trotsky was also a mathematician.
- He forged his name to Trotsky when he forged his passport during his escape to Siberia. It is a German word meaning defiance.
- He was the initiator of concentration camps and compulsory labour camps.

LUIZ INÁCIO LULA DA SILVA

President of Brazil, Luiz Inacio Lula da Silva, has been called the most popular politician of the world by the US President, Barack Obama.

EARLY LIFE

Luiz Inacio Lula da Silva was born on 27 October 1945 in Caetes, Brazil. Born in a poor family, he learnt the value of being content with whatever one had. He worked as a shoeshine boy, a street vendor and even in small factories. Lula couldn't continue with his studies after grade five, and started working in a warehouse at fourteen.

EARLY CAREER

Lula's brother inspired him to join labour movements. This led to Lula finding his calling in understanding and expressing the concerns of the other workers. Soon, he was seen organizing labour activities and protests as well. He became the union president and started a campaign against the government and demanded increase in wages. This got him national attention.

JOINING POLITICS

In 1980, Lula, along with others, founded the Workers' Party. Lula realized that until he was on the other side of the government, he wouldn't be able to usher in the required changes. Therefore, Lula sought to run for the post of the governor of his state but lost. Resolute, he ran for the highest post of the country, that of president, three times, only to lose every time but for the last! He won the presidential elections in 2002 on the basis of a campaign that included not only a promise to uplift the poor but also to provide opportunities to people from all walks of life.

PRESIDENTSHIP

Lula served as the president the second time in 2006. The government's priorities were to end corruption, improve economy and initiate certain reforms. Lula was concerned about improving the conditions of fifty million Brazilians living below the poverty line. He is said to have alleviated the poverty of more than twenty million people.

Lula's governance also witnessed a growth in the number of foreign policies. More than forty Brazilian embassies opened around the world. He extended ties with the other countries of Latin America, Africa, Middle East and several parts of the Asian world. He also undertook many social projects benefitting the poor, like removing hunger, increasing food and kitchen gas allowance, providing affordable housing schemes, etc.

Lula won the affection of his people as he brought general well-being into the lives of the people. He was successful in uniting South America. Brazil had built a road to peace and harmony among the Latin Americans.

Since the constitution did not allow the president to run for a third consecutive term, Lula could not do so. But Lula still remains a powerful figure in Brazil.

DID YOU KNOW?

- At the age of nineteen, Lula lost his little finger while working in an automobile parts manufacturing company and had to run from pillar to post for medical attention. This incident drove him to join the workers' union.
- Lula was a close friend of the former Cuban president, Fidel Castro. Castro helped and advised him during his presidential elections.
- *Time* magazine voted Lula as one of the '100 Most Influential People in the World'.

MAHATHIR MOHAMAD

Mahathir Mohamad is a physician, statesman and author who is serving his second stint as the Prime Minister of Malaysia. He has indeed given a new status to Malaysia in the world map.

EARLY LIFE
Mahathir Mohamad was born in a humble family on 10 July 1925 in Alor Setar, a rural town in Malaya. His father was a school teacher. Mohamad was a bright student and learnt to read the Quran from his mother. As a 16-year-old boy, he witnessed the Second World War. After his regular schooling, he joined the medical school at the University of Malaya in Singapore.

ENTERING POLITICS
After receiving his medical degree, Mahathir worked as a government service doctor until 1956. Then, he joined politics. He joined several political parties including the United Malays National Organization (UMNO). He was elected to the parliament as a member of UMNO in 1964 and ran for his first political position. However, he could not enjoy it for long as he had to resign, became he had angered the prime minister, Tunku Abdul Rahman by demanding equal status of the Malays and the Chinese. He stayed away from politics for three years. He joined back in 1974 and became the education minister.

BECOMING THE PRIME MINISTER AND REVOLUTIONIZING MALAYSIA
On 16 July 1981, he was sworn in as the prime minister. The first two years were extremely difficult because there were frequent conflicts with the royal family.

Mahathir is considered the father of modern Malaysia who led the country's progress for over two decades. He lay down a plan for Malaysia where priorities, plans and results were pre-determined. He directed a major part of the state fund to education, training of craftsmen, English teaching and research, and opened Islamic universities. He also started scholarships for meritorious students who wished to study abroad.

Mahathir wanted to make the Malays self-reliant. He knew that changes had to be made at the grassroots level for any significant change. Perhaps what endeared him to his people was his complete transparency regarding his plans and strategies. He also revealed all his accounting systems and developed a unique way of motivating the people by following the method of reward and punishment.

MAJOR DECISIONS

Mahathir knew that he had to tap the economy of the country and he began by focusing on agriculture. Malaysia is suitable for palm cultivation and he planted one million palm seedlings. Soon Malaysia became one of the first countries to export palm oil. He invested on improving the road and transport of the country to encourage tourism.

The per capita income grew, and the unemployment level fell as low as 3 per cent under his leadership. The world waits to see Malaysia achieve new glories under Mahathir's sensible leadership.

DID YOU KNOW?

- Mahathir Mohamad was the first Malay doctor to set up a clinic in Malaysia.
- He dreaded his teacher Mr Hassan during his school days as he used to either pinch or use the ruler to punish a child in case of mistakes.
- His first book, *The Malay Dilemma*, was banned by the government as, according to them, it contained radical ideas.

MAHATMA GANDHI

Mahatma Gandhi is an international symbol of peace and human rights, an inspiration to people around the world, the architect of non-violence civil disobedience and a major contributor to India's independence. He is fondly known as Bapu.

EARLY LIFE

On 2 October 1869, Mohandas Gandhi was born into the modest business family of Karamchand Gandhi. His family wanted him to pursue a legal career and thus sent him in 1888 to study law in London. He returned to India in 1891.

SOUTH AFRICA AND GANDHI

Gandhi went to South Africa to begin his legal career in 1893. On arriving there, he was appalled by the gross discrimination meted out to Indians by the British. The incident of him being thrown out of a train despite having a first class ticket, because he was an Indian, triggered him to fight against colour prejudice. He organized the Indian community staying there to oppose racial discrimination without the use of violence. He stayed in South Africa for twenty years, and during this period, he was arrested about six times for voicing his protest against the South African government. His major achievements in South Africa were the recognition of Hindu marriage and the abolition of the poll tax levied on Indians. On his return to India, Gandhi called for mass boycotts and asked people to stop working for the crown. He urged people to be self-reliant, and his spinning wheel became the symbol of Indian independence.

THE SALT MARCH

Gandhi organized the revolutionary Salt March in 1930 to protest against the British Salt Act which prohibited people from collecting or selling salt. It also imposed a heavy tax on the Indians. As a mark of protest, Gandhi marched 390 km to the Arabian Sea which took twenty-three days.

FREEDOM OF INDIA

Gandhi assumed leadership of the Indian National Congress in 1920 and gave it up in 1934, passing it on to Jawaharlal Nehru. He focused on education, poverty, sanitation, etc. In 1942, Gandhi launched the Quit India Movement demanding the British to leave the country. Gandhi played an important role in the negotiations between the two nations regarding the matters pertaining to independence.

Freedom came to the Indians but with the heavy price of partition. There were communal riots between the Hindus and the Muslims. Gandhiji tried his level best to stop the bloodshed but nothing much could be done. He even fasted for many days to end the violence.

GANDHI'S ASSASSINATION

In the winter of 1948, on 30 January, as the 78-year-old Gandhi was walking towards his prayer meeting, Nathuram Godse fired three shots at him at point-blank range. This violent act shook the world and was the end of the journey of a great soul.

LEGACY

Gandhi has inspired freedom fighters across the globe such as Martin Luther King Jr and Nelson Mandela. The world will be indebted to him for introducing them to the concept of Satyagragha which remains one of the most efficacious philosophies in freedom struggles today. He always wore a simple loincloth and shawl. Because of his values, he came to be known as the 'Mahatma', which means 'great soul'.

DID YOU KNOW?

- Gandhi had very bad handwriting and was often scolded by his teachers for this.
- He was responsible for civil rights movements in four continents and twelve countries.
- Fifty-three roads in India and forty-eight outside are named after him.

MAHINDA RAJAPAKSA

Mahinda Rajapaksa is a great statesman whom Sri Lanka looks up to for its development. He is a progressive leader who aims to resolve the various differences prevailing in the country.

EARLY LIFE

Mahinda Rajapaksa was born into a prominent political family in the district of Hambantota of Sri Lanka on 18 November 1945. His father fought for independence and was later the cabinet minister of agriculture. He was drawn to the political affairs of the country from a very young age, as his uncle, D.M. Rajapaksa, who championed the cause of the cultivators in his area, had a strong influence upon him. This resulted in his entering politics quite early in life. Defending his lack of high education, he wittily says that politicians come from the University of Life and therefore need to have experience in politics. However, he entered a law college later as a member of the parliament and earned a degree in law.

ENTERING POLITICS

The sudden demise of his father resulted in Rajapaksa joining politics early, as he had to fill his father's place to contest elections. Rajapaksa entered politics in 1970 when he was only twenty-four years old. However, it was only an official entry as he had entered politics ideologically at a young age. The young Rajapaksa was known as an advocate of human rights, and this would forever remain his guiding principle. Having lost the seat in 1977, he started focusing on his law career before re-entering the parliament in 1989. Serving as the labour minister and the minister of fisheries and aquatic resources under President Chandrika Kumaratunga, he soon became the 13th prime minister of Sri Lanka.

PRESIDENCY

Kumaratunga saw all the qualities of an able leader in Rajapaksa and thus endorsed him as her successor. He was elected as the president in 2005 which was a crucial year for Sri Lanka as the country was holding peace talks and discussing a precarious ceasefire agreement with Liberation Tigers of Tamil Eelam (LTTE), the guerrilla organization that sought to establish an independent Tamil state in northern and eastern Sri Lanka.

However, Rajapaksa announced his intention to eradicate the separatist group which had been operating as a rebel army and de facto government in many parts of Sri Lanka. The country's armed forces led their battle against the LTTE, ultimately defeating the rebels and killing their leader, Velupillai Prabhakaran.

ENDING CIVIL WAR

Sri Lanka had been reeling under the clouds of civil war for more than twenty years. Rajapaksa, without bothering about his international image, ended the civil war which was the biggest hurdle towards the country's growth and development. He declared a war against terrorism and attained total victory on 18 May 2009. Although there have been many allegations of war crimes against him, he has no regrets for the strong decisions that he had to take for his country's welfare.

OTHER CONTRIBUTIONS

The end of terrorism in Sri Lanka led to the opening of several venues for development. Rajapaksa took upon himself the great challenge of reconstructing the country. He turned all his attention to develop the country's trade, tourism and infrastructure. The life expectancy, per capita income and education also improved under his leadership.

He initiated, developed and completed many highways and also boosted tourism. The Colombo beautification project took care of many rural infrastructure projects.

Rajapaksa is a proud Sinhalese. He is identified with development and improvement in life in Sri Lanka.

DID YOU KNOW?

- Since most men in Rajapaksa's family did not live long, Rajapaksa takes utmost care of his health and undergoes check-ups almost every day.
- He has earned the moniker 'Lord of the rings', as he wears a number of rings and talismans.
- There is a road named after Rajapaksa in Palestine as an expression of gratitude towards his contribution to the struggle of the Palestinians.

MALALA YOUSAFZAI

Malala Yousafzai is the youngest activist of the world. She is an epitome of inner strength and a crusader for women's education.

EARLY LIFE

Malala Yousafzai was born on 12 July 1997 in Mingora, Pakistan. It was a peaceful town until the Taliban tried to take control of it. Her father was a progressive person and celebrated the birth of his daughter even though the birth of a girl was never a matter of happiness there. He also opened a school after the birth of Malala. As a child, Malala wanted to become a doctor but her father inspired her to enter politics. She grew up listening to the tales of statesmanship and was inspired to express her views against the atrocities of the Taliban from her father.

FIGHT FOR EDUCATION

Malala was extremely upset when the Taliban objected to girls' education. She considered this to be a violation of her fundamental right. Thus began her journey of protests and the tribulations associated with it. She used to write her feelings in a diary which were brought to light when a BBC journalist found in Malala the person who could fearlessly narrate the life of people in Swat Valley facing the atrocities of the Taliban. The eleven-years-old emerged as a voice for the victims of suppression. She began writing under the name Gul Makai and would send all her notes to the BBC, but then the Yousafzai family had to flee from the Swat Valley.

TALIBAN RETALIATION

The writings of Malala caused such a furore and anger among the Taliban that there was a fight in the Swat Valley between the Taliban and the Pakistan Army. The tremendous fight led to the taking over of the area by the Pakistan Army.

Many people, including Malala's family, who had fled from Swat Valley, returned. Malala had gained popularity as a young activist who did not fear speaking the truth. She appeared in interviews in many news channels. Her appeal was for providing enough opportunities for women's education. She received the International Children Peace Prize in 2011, the first Pakistani to receive this award.

ASSASSINATION ATTEMPT

Malala's public profile was growing along with the danger that loomed over her head because of the Taliban. She received continuous death threats on her Facebook profile. But Malala was certainly not one to be deterred by them. On 9 October 2012, when Malala was returning home after her exams in her school bus, a masked terrorist boarded the school bus and demanded to know which of them was Malala. Then, exhibiting great courage, she stood up and said, 'I am Malala.' She was shot in her head.

GREAT SURVIVOR

Malala underwent surgeries and treatment at Peshawar Military Hospital and later she was flown to Britain. She recovered after five major surgeries and received good wishes from all over the world. The Right to Education for women was passed as a bill after protests against the Taliban poured in from all over the world.

Malala was the youngest person to receive the Nobel Peace Prize in 2014. She stands tall as a source of motivation and staunch courage to all.

DID YOU KNOW?

- Malala has received around forty awards and honours for her bravery and activism.
- An asteroid was named in honour of Malala in 2015.

MALCOLM X

Malcolm X is one of the most significant personalities in American black history; someone for whom the Afro-Americans have a lot of respect. He is remembered as a fiery civil activist leader.

EARLY LIFE

Malcolm X was born as Malcolm Little on 19 May 1925 in Omaha, Nebraska. He was born to a preacher, Earl Little, and a homemaker. His father was also an activist and spoke out against racism. Due to this, the family had to face atrocities including being targeted by the Ku Klux Klan, a group formed by white southerners to crush African-American leaders.

There was so much resistance against Earl Little that they had to move to a new place, Milwaukee. However, the family had to undergo the pain of Earl Little being murdered in 1931 which was devastating for the whole family. Malcolm's mother became ill and the children were placed in foster care.

Life at a foster home was not good for Malcolm because he wanted to be treated like a human being and not a pet. Although he excelled in school, there was not much scope for African-Americans and so he dropped out of school at fifteen. He moved in with his half sister, Ella, who taught him the lesson of self-esteem and pride.

TURNING POINT

Moving from one place to another made him take up several jobs for his living. But when Malcolm fell into bad company, he was given ten years imprisonment for dealing with drugs. In prison, he turned to books and was drawn to Islam. He joined the Nation of Islam (NOI), a movement that ensured the recognition of blacks. Malcolm was inspired by the talks and teachings of Elijah Muhammad. He then changed his name to Malcolm X as a representation of his lost association with Africa. Soon he became an important leader of the NOI. He was made the national spokesman of NOI. Its membership increased from a mere 500 to 30,000 under him.

JOINING CIVIL RIGHTS MOVEMENT

Malcolm X was a gifted orator and he persuaded the blacks to rise up for nationalism through any means. By then, Martin Luther King Jr had become a significant figure of the civil rights movement. However, Malcolm did not agree with him in terms of ideologies. While Martin Luther was all for peace and non-violent methods, Malcolm said that no revolution could be successful without violent methods. These radical thoughts attracted the attention of the whites and he was seen as a threat. But his powerful voice as a significant speaker of civil rights continued to gain momentum. His clarion call to all his people was to fight against racism. He was such powerful voice that even those who disagreed with him respected him.

RENOUNCING NATION OF ISLAM

Malcolm X left the Nation of Islam as he was disillusioned by Elijah Muhamad whom he had considered to be his mentor. He founded the religious organization, The Muslim Mosque, and went to Mecca on a pilgrimage. It was an eye-opener for him as he witnessed, for the first time, so many people of different races united by the same faith.

SPIRITUAL AWAKENING

The pilgrimage to Mecca changed Malcolm completely. He was less angry and finally realized that it might be possible to have a bloodless revolution. However, it's tragic that when he thought of changing his path to peaceful ways, he was assassinated on 21 February 1965. He will always be remembered for igniting the desire for freedom in the common man.

DID YOU KNOW?

- Malcolm dropped out of school when his white teacher told him that his dream of becoming a lawyer was not realistic for a 'nigger'.
- Muhammad Ali, the heavyweight champion, was inspired by Malcolm to change his religion and become a member of the Nation of Islam.
- The FBI kept a close watch on him from 1950 till his death.

MAO TSE-TUNG

M ao Tse-Tung is hailed as one of history's greatest revolutionary leaders. A multifaceted personality, he is known as the father of the Chinese Cultural Revolution.

EARLY LIFE
Mao Tse-Tung was born to a farmer's family on 26 December 1893 in the Hunan Province of China. His father, Mao Yichang, was initially a poor farmer who eventually became prosperous. In 1918, Mao spent a very brief period of time in Peking where he broadened his view of the world. By the time Mao returned to Hunan, in 1919, he was a devout follower of communism.

ENTERING POLITICS
Inspired by Marx's class struggle and Lenin's anti-imperialist stand, Mao began a rigorous exploration of political and economic affairs. He edited radical magazines, organized trade unions and also established politically-oriented schools of his own. He also embraced socialist ideals.

Following a violent crackdown by Chiang Kai-shek, a military leader as well as the heir to the Chinese President, Sun Yat-sen, in September, Mao Tse-Tung led an army of peasants against the Kuomintang (Chinese Nationalist Party), a rival of the communists. He was eventually defeated, and the remaining army fled to Jiangxi Province. In the mountainous area of Jiangxi, Mao established the Soviet Republic of China where he was elected as the chairman. By the year 1934, the communists controlled more than ten regions, which made Chiang nervous.

COMING TO POWER
In 1937, the Japanese Imperial Army invaded China and Chiang Kai-

shek was forced to flee to Nanking. Within no time, Chiang's forces also lost control of coastal regions and major cities and reached out to the communists. Mao fought the Japanese with support from the Allied forces, which then helped him establish himself as a credible military leader.

Mao defeated the Japanese in 1945 and was positioned to control all of China. On 1 October 1949, Mao seized the opportunity and announced the establishment of the People's Republic of China.

CONTRIBUTION

After taking control of China, Mao Tse-Tung handed lands owned by warlords to people's communes. He also helped enhance the status of women, set up schools and improved access to healthcare. Since Mao's reforms were largely restricted to the rural areas, this led to some discontent in the cities.

Soon after, Mao Tse-Tung tried a new model to boost agricultural and industrial production, called the 'Great Leap Forward'. The plan failed due to poor planning, and in 1959, Mao Tse-Tung relinquished the chairmanship of the People's Republic of China.

RETURN TO POWER

Mao Tse-Tung returned to the political centre stage in 1966 and launched the Cultural Revolution in a classic autocratic method. Mao informed his followers that the bourgeois were trying to restore capitalism and ordered them to be removed from society. His diktat included closure of China's schools and sending young intellectuals from the cities to the countryside to re-educate themselves in hard manual labour. This cultural evolution created economic and social chaos. It was around this time that Mao created a cult around his personality, made possible by the adulation of the Red Guards, a paramilitary movement of students led by Mao.

Due to his influence on the Chinese nation, many in China equate Mao Tse-Tung with Qin Shi-Huang, the first emperor who unified China in 221 BC. Mao Tse-Tung harnessed the agrarian discontent and nationalism, and transformed a tiny band of peasants into an army of millions who fought for around twenty years against the government led by the Kuomintang party to finally taste victory.

Mao Tse-Tung died from Parkinson's disease on 9 September 1976. Chinese history holds him in high regard as a great political strategist and military mastermind for China's late 20th century development.

DID YOU KNOW?

- Mao Tse-Tung was an accomplished poet and writer in the ancient Chinese classical style.
- He launched the famous '100 Flowers Campaign' which allowed people the freedom of expression.
- Even though he was an accomplished fighter, Mao Tse-Tung was afraid of flying.

MARGARET THATCHER

Margaret Thatcher was the first female prime minister of Britain. She was a non-compromising idealist and was rightly referred to as the Iron Lady.

EARLY LIFE
Margaret Hilda Roberts was born on 13 October 1925 to Alfred Roberts and Beatrice Ethel. She did her schooling from Grantham Girls' High School and was a meritorious student actively participating in various extracurricular activities. She studied chemistry at Oxford University. After earning her degree in 1947, she worked as a research scientist. It is amazing to note that during her free time she started studying law and eventually passed the bar.

INROAD TO POLITICS
Margaret imbibed her interest in politics from her father who was a conservative and a mayor. Even though she lost the Dartford parliamentary seat in 1950, she made an impact on people by her powerful speeches.

EMERGENCE OF A LEADER
The Conservative Party came into power in 1970. Thatcher was appointed the secretary of state for education and science. It is said that she was frustrated at various points because she had to struggle to prove that despite being a woman she was equally capable as a man.

Margaret Thatcher created history when she was elected as the first female prime minister of Britain in 1979 with the coming of the conservatives into power.

EMERGENCE OF A NEW ERA
Britain was merely a shadow of its previous glorious self when

she became the prime minister. To tackle inflation, she took the strong measure of privatizing social housing and public transport. She also made some changes in the taxation policies and reduced government spending.

Thatcher ushered in a sense of pride for her country by winning the Falklands War where she had sent troops to defend the British island. It was the first military victory since 1945. This made her a popular leader and she went on to become the prime minister for the second time in 1983.

SECOND INNINGS

Thatcher made a remarkable change in the working of the people. She welcomed the era of popular capitalism and denationalized many state monopolies. Her tremendous success lay in making it possible for establishing many small businesses which later formed the foundation of the economy of the country.

Privatization encouraged foreign investors to invest there. Lowered taxes, lesser strikes at factories and an increased GDP ensured that the country was working towards an era of growth. Companies like the British Airways and Rolls Royce which had been running on losses were now making profits.

THIRD AND FINAL INNINGS

Margaret Thatcher had become a name to be reckoned with in world politics. She was elected as the prime minister for the third time in 1987. After coming to power, she worked towards implementing a standard educational curriculum across the nation.

On 22 November 1990, Margaret Thatcher submitted her resignation and said that the interests of the party were of higher priority than her own. When she failed to get a majority, she took it as a cue that she had to gracefully exit for making way for other leaders.

DEATH AND LEGACY

The death of Margaret Thatcher's husband Denis Thatcher and her dear friend Ronald Reagan were major setbacks for her. She gave up public and political life completely in 2011 and breathed her last on 8 April 2013. She is best remembered as someone who gave a new lease of life to the failing economy of Britain.

DID YOU KNOW?

- Thatcher loved to read poetry and her favourite poet was Rudyard Kipling.
- Her life has been captured in the movie *The Iron Lady* and her role was enacted by the famous Hollywood actress Meryl Streep.
- She used to love to play the piano.

MARTIN LUTHER KING JR

Martin Luther King Jr was a leader in the true sense of the term. A name intertwined with the civil rights movement in the US, he showed the world the power of non-violence.

EARLY LIFE

Martin Luther King Jr was born Michael Luther King Jr but later he changed his name to Martin. He attended segregated public schools in Georgia and graduated from high school at the age of fifteen. In 1948, he received his BA degree from Morehouse College, a distinguished histrically black college of Atlanta.

During his three years of theological study at Crozer Theological Seminary in Pennsylvania, he was elected president of a predominantly white senior class. In 1951, he was awarded the Bachelor of Divinity. With a fellowship, which he had won at Crozer, he enrolled in graduate studies at Boston University, completing his residence for the doctorate in 1953 and receiving the degree in 1955.

SPIRITUAL CALLING

King's spiritual development was much influenced by Benjamin E. Mays, an educator, minister and civil rights leader, who inspired him to use religion to promote racial equality and social change. He settled in Alabama and became the twentieth pastor of the Dexter Avenue Baptist Church. He professed tolerance and non-violence.

CIVIL RIGHTS MOVEMENT

The refusal of Rosa Parks to give up her bus seat kindled the flame of the civil rights movement in the US. King had a major role to play in the movement. The boycott of buses in Montgomery was extremely successful because he worked shoulder to shoulder with the people and made them realize that they wouldn't allow that kind of discrimination to continue.

BIRTH OF A LEADER

The bold step of boycotting buses for 381 days made King emerge as a leader of the coloured community and also led to the landmark decision by the Supreme Court on 20 December 1956 stating that segregation of buses on the basis of colour was unconstitutional. This was a tremendous victory not only towards the cause of civil rights but also for the fact that King's non-violent ways could yield results. People reposed their faith on him and soon King became the national face of civil rights. King left no stone unturned to further his cause. He was jailed for over twenty times and was also stabbed in the chest. Not only this, his house was bombed and his family suffered too. His family and children extended their support to the cause and showed to the world that they would not think twice before laying down their lives for it. King realized that he wouldn't be able to take the fight forward alone without the support of the people. Therefore, he travelled from 1957 to 1968 and delivered around 2,500 speeches, including the better known 'I have a dream' speech in 1963. He also authored five books and wrote dozens of articles. President John F. Kennedy met him personally.

SAD DEMISE

In the spring of 1968, King went to Memphis to extend his support for black sanitation workers who faced discrimination. He delivered the rousing speech 'I have been to the mountain top' which proved to be his last. On April 4, while he was standing at the balcony of his motel, he was shot and killed.

DID YOU KNOW?

- The third Monday of every January is celebrated as Martin Luther King Jr Day.
- King donated the entire amount of his prize money for his Nobel Peace Prize towards the cause of civil rights.
- Over 700 streets across the US are named after him.

MAUMOON ABDUL GAYOOM

Maumoon Abdul Gayoom, five times president of the Maldives, transformed his country from a small fishing island to a paradise. A man of indomitable spirit, he holds the record of being the longest-serving president in Asia.

EARLY LIFE

Maumoon Abdul Gayoom was born on 29 December 1937 to Abdul Gayoom Ibrahim and Khadeeja in the Maldives. His family was fairly wealthy. He received his education from Egypt where he spent six months learning Arabic before joining school. He graduated in 1966. He also learnt English there.

EARLY CAREER

After his graduation, Gayoom joined a university in Nigeria as a professor of Islamic Studies. He returned to the Maldives in 1971 and joined a school, teaching English, Arithmetic and Islam. However, he had to leave his job as he was placed under house arrest for criticizing the president's insensitivity towards human rights.

Gayoom was appointed as the undersecretary in the telecommunications department and soon he was promoted to the post of the director. But he did not give up teaching, and joined some private schools as a part-time teacher. In 1975, he was sent to the UN as part of a delegation representing the Maldives.

PRESIDENT OF THE MALDIVES

When Gayoom was serving as the minister of transport, he emerged as one of the frontrunners for the presidential elections owing to his capability and knowledge. He was elected as the president of Maldives in 1978 with a staggering 92.96 per cent votes.

When Gayoom became the president, there were very few

government schools in the Maldives, but today there are more than 100 schools, thanks to his efforts. The health sector also witnessed a tremendous change with a rise in the number of hospitals and doctors.

Since tourism is the backbone of Maldives's economy, he turned the country into a tourist-friendly place. Today, the country is visited by over a million tourists every year. The Maldives has become one of the most prosperous nations in South East Asia because of tourism.

GAYOOM, THE ENVIRONMENTALIST

Gayoom was aware of the rising tide of the Indian Ocean and understood that gradually Maldives would go under water if environment was not taken care of. Gayoom has said that each country and individual in the world has to take up the responsibility of safeguarding the environment. Climate change is a universal problem and therefore requires an all-inclusive universal solution. He believes that vulnerable countries must quickly tap resources and use assistance to combat climate change.

2008 ELECTIONS

Gayoom lost the presidential elections to Mohamed Nasheed in 2008. He continued to be in the Opposition but retired from active politics in 2010. But, he could not stay away from politics for long and returned in September 2011 as the leader of the newly-formed Progressive Party of Maldives (PPM). He is still considered a great influence in the Maldives.

DID YOU KNOW?

- Gayoom has turned a cluster of desert coral reef islands into ultimate holiday destinations.
- Three attempts were made to overthrow his government, and in the third attempt, he took the help of the Indian military to curb the resistance.

MICHELLE BACHELET

Michelle Bachelet is the first female elected president of Chile. She is like the phoenix who rose from the ashes more resolute and strong after every failure that she experienced in life.

EARLY LIFE

Verónica Michelle Bachelet Jeria was born on 29 September 1951 in Santiago, Chile. Her father was a general in Chile's air force while her mother was an archaeologist. She spent her childhood moving from one military base to another. She was a bright student and completed her high school from Chile. Besides studies, she was also interested in volleyball and theatre. Her leadership qualities were evident from childhood.

Life changed for her completely when her father was arrested for opposing a military coup that brought General Augusto Pinochet to power. He died of heart attack in custody in 1974. Bachelet was arrested along with her mother and sent to a secret prison where they were tortured and interrogated. Later, they were exiled. She returned to Chile in 1979 and completed her studies.

ENTERING POLITICS

It was difficult for Bachelet to find work in Chile after completion of her studies. However, this did not stop her from becoming active in politics and developing socialist views. In 2000, she was appointed the minister for health and helped introduce many reforms. Her appointment as the minister for national defence in 2002 was a landmark achievement because she was the first woman to hold this high post. She was the main force behind the modernization of the Chilean armed forces.

PRESIDENCY

Bachelet was emerging as a national leader. Her popularity kept growing and she was considered an able candidate for the presidency. She was freed from her government post so that she could start with her campaign. The main agendas of her campaign were providing free healthcare for old people and bringing reforms in the social and electoral system. She won the 2006 elections and became the first female president in Latin America. She was sworn into office. Her cabinet consisted of an equal number of men and women.

True to her words, she passed a new legislation that guaranteed minimum pension for the 60 per cent poor population. Her legislation of equal pay for equal work, both in the public and the private sector, as well as between men and women, was applauded by all. She also reformed the laws regarding providing comprehensive social services to children. She provided books to about 4,00,000 poor families and free computers to poor students of the seventh grade performing well in academics. During her years in office, the economy grew rapidly, unemployment reduced and the rate of poverty also came down. Bachelet was sworn in as the president for the second time on 11 March 2014. This time, she brought about certain tax reforms and also brought forth the environmental policies that saved around 142 endemic marine species, some of which were nearing extinction.

Five new national parks and nine marine reserves were also created to protect the biodiversity of the country. She created a new ministry for women and gender equality.

POPULARITY

Michelle Bachelet has become a symbol of the emancipation of women in Latin America. She urges women to participate more in all sectors to empower themselves.

DID YOU KNOW?

- Bachelet created a 2,86,000-square-mile marine reserve around Easter Island for the protection of endemic species.
- She never wanted to be the president, and she accepted the nomination only because she did not want to disappoint her supporters.
- She opened eighteen new subway stations in Santiago.

MIKHAIL GORBACHEV

Mikhail Gorbachev is still the most renowned name in Russia that has had the highest influence on its history. His unique leadership lies in the fact that he managed to be a liberal leader among the leftist and rightist leaders.

EARLY LIFE

Mikhail Sergeyevich Gorbachev was born on 2 March 1931 in Privolnoye, Russia. His parents were ordinary peasants. He was a meritorious child, and traits of leadership were seen in him from a young age.

Attracted to the ideology of communism, he joined 'Komsomol' (Young Communist League) in 1941. The World War had left an indelible mark on him. He attained a law degree in 1955 and later held many different positions in Komsomol and even became the first secretary of the regional party committee in 1970.

ENTERING POLITICS

Gorbachev gave up his job as a lawyer to join Komsomol. In 1950, Soviet was passing through a political turmoil. There was great oppression by the communists and cold war with other countries. Gorbachev did not agree and appreciate the ways of Stalin and fearlessly expressed them. There was a time when he was losing hope in the politics of the country.

However, with the demise of Stalin in 1953, things changed for Gorbachev. In 1970, he became the first secretary of the Stavropol Territorial Committee which was the highest executive body of the government. This proved to be a stepping stone for him to be recognized at the national level.

In 1978, he took over the responsibilities of agricultural administration. By 1980, Gorbachev became a member of the politburo, the small group comprising of top communist leaders.

The Soviet Union was passing through an economic stagnation which had started in the late sixties and continued till 1982. Gorbachev was not happy with the way in which the country was being governed. He thought that he would finally be able to improve things, as his role in governance expanded, but he found the system very rigid to change.

LEADER WITH A DIFFERENCE
Gorbachev was unanimously elected to power in 1990 as the first president of the Soviet Union. The Russians expected him to reform the system. He planned new policies to regenerate the system. His walking down the streets with his wife and meeting people from all walks of life was a common sight.

ESTABLISHING FOREIGN RELATIONS
Gorbachev knew that the Soviet could not isolate itself from others. To progress, he had to establish friendly relations with the outside world. He met Ronald Reagan, the president of the US. The two leaders took a stand that nuclear war should never be fought.

FACING HURDLES
Gorbachev initiated many political changes in the country. The most significant was ending the Soviet military occupation in Afghanistan. Although appreciated by the world, he faced problems within his own country.

There were people from different ethnic groups and they started demanding independence. The industrial and the agricultural systems were declining. He made all the information of the atrocities during the time of Stalin available to the public. It found appreciation in a faction of people while many objected to it too. By now, Gorbachev was disillusioned about the one-party system and how it was curbing all development.

In 1988, Gorbachev convinced other communist leaders to

go for contested elections, which was announcing the end of the communist system. He also introduced free speech in the country. The collapse of the Soviet Union had begun. In a way, he released the country from the bondage of totalitarianism and ushered in the dawn of democracy.

DID YOU KNOW?

- As a ten-year-old boy, Gorbachev appeared in a television advertisement on pizza.
- He won a Grammy award in the Spoken World Album in the children's category.
- He won the Noble Peace Prize in 1990 for his role in establishing peace in the world.

MOTHER TERESA

Mother Teresa is an iconic personality and a symbol of unconditional love, charity and selfless service. She is a name to reckon with in the world for her outstanding humanitarian work.

EARLY LIFE

She was born on 26 August 1910 and baptized as Agnes Gonxha Bojaxhiu. Her parents, Nikolle and Dranafile Bojaxhiu, were devout Catholics of Albanian descent. Imbibing the compassionate nature from her mother, Agnes decided to be a nun. She took the name Sister Mary Teresa after Saint Thérèse of Lisieux in the Sisters of Loreto congregation in Dublin.

Sister Teresa came to Calcutta (not Kolkata) in May 1931 to teach poor and destitute girls. She took her final profession of vows to a life of poverty, chastity and obedience on 24 May 1937. Thereupon, she took the title of 'Mother' and came to be known as Mother Teresa. She strived to lead people to a life of devotion to Christ through her kindness and love.

MOTHER TERESA'S 'CALL WITHIN A CALL'

Mother Teresa experienced, what she calls a 'call within a call' in 1946 when Christ directed her to give up teaching and dedicate her life to the cause of the poor and the destitute. Henceforth, she decided to work for the slum dwellers of Calcutta. Donning her trademark blue and white saree, she finally started to attend to this new calling in 1948. She went into the alleys of the slums with only one aim, that is to care for the uncared and love the unloved.

THE MISSIONARIES OF CHARITY

Mother Teresa began an open-air school and also established a home for the dying destitute in a dilapidated building in Calcutta. Her selfless service attracted many, and by 1950, she had established 'The Missionaries of Charity' to 'care for the hungry, the naked, the homeless and the crippled'. She also established Nirmal Hriday, a home for the poor and dying, Shanti Nagar for the lepers and Nirmala Shishu Bhavan for the homeless children. By the year 1960, owing largely to donations and other kinds of help, she had opened orphanages and leper houses across India.

INTERNATIONAL CHARITY

Mother Teresa also opened help centres in Venezuela, Tanzania, Italy, Austria and many more countries. The year 1963 saw the foundation of 'The Missionaries of Charity Brothers' and 'The Missionary of Charity Fathers' in 1984 with the objective of extending her philanthropic cause to the entire world. By 2007, the Missionaries of Charity had 600 missions, schools and shelters in 120 countries.

Mother Teresa was now able to reach out to the victims of natural disasters like earthquake, famine, and also war victims. Criticism or praise did not affect her relentless humanitarian service.

WANING HEALTH AND DEMISE

Two heart attacks in 1983 and 1989 respectively left her physically weak and with an artificial pacemaker. She also suffered from pneumonia and malaria. Her resignation from The Missionaries of Charity was not accepted though.

RECOGNITION AND AWARDS

Mother Teresa got recognition in India and abroad too. She was awarded the Padma Shri in 1962 and the Jawaharlal Nehru Award for International Understanding in 1966. She also received the Bharat Ratna. Mother Teresa received the Ramon Magsaysay Award for Peace and International Understanding, which is given for humanitarian work in South and East Asia. Her ultimate recognition was the love and respect of the people that she earned across the world.

CANONIZATION

Mother Teresa left for her heavenly abode on 5 September 1997 and was declared a saint as there were evidences that she could perform miracles. She was canonized by Pope Francis on 4 September 2016 in St Peter's Square in the Vatican City.

DID YOU KNOW?

- Mother Teresa never met her mother and sister after she became a nun.
- She refused the traditional Nobel honour banquet and instead requested that the allotted budget ($1,92,000) be given to help the poor in India.
- After receiving the Nobel Peace Prize, she said, 'I am unworthy'.

MUHAMMAD ALI JINNAH

Muhammad Ali Jinnah, an able statesman and adept diplomat, is popularly known as the father of Pakistan.

EARLY LIFE

Jinnah was born on 25 December 1876 in Karachi which was a part of British India. His father was a prosperous merchant. After his schooling from Karachi Madrassa School and a Christian missionary school, he joined the honourable society of Lincoln's Inn in 1893 in London, England. He found his calling and became the youngest Indian to be called to the bar in England. He returned to India after his studies and started practising in Bombay.

ENTRY INTO POLITICS

During his stay in London, Jinnah often visited the House of Commons and developed a liking for politics. After returning to India, he started working for a better representation of India in the British Parliament.

Jinnah joined the Indian National Congress in 1906 and also served as a secretary to Dadabhai Naoroji, the then Congress president.

In 1910, Jinnah was elected to the newly constituted imperial legislative council. He was a powerful voice of the Indian cause and Indian rights. He gradually emerged as a prominent voice of India and also of Hindu-Muslim unity. In fact, it was Jinnah who led to the signing of the pact between the All-India Muslim League and the Indian National Congress in 1916 which gave the All-India Muslim League the right to be a representative of all the Muslims of the country.

INDEPENDENT PAKISTAN

Jinnah was devastated by the rising violence between the Hindus and the Muslims. He left the Congress in 1920 after the Nagpur session because Jinnah could not agree with Gandhi's ideologies and felt that they would aggravate the distrust between the two religions. He started nurturing the thought that the only way to preserve the Muslim heritage and political interests was to have a separate nation for the Muslims in the Indian subcontinent.

Jinnah proposed the partition of India in 1940 in a meeting of the Muslim League at Lahore. He believed that Muslims would be treated as second-class citizens in India, a surprise for both the Hindus and the British.

Sadly, the distance between the two religions grew wider which led to the eruption of violent communal riots across the nation. Lord Mountbatten was sent to India to negotiate with both the parties and pass the power to two successive states, India and Pakistan, on 15 August 1947. Pakistan was carved out of the Muslim dominant region of northwest India and Bengal in the east. The Muslim League declared Jinnah as the governor general of independent Pakistan.

LAYING THE FOUNDATION

Governing Pakistan was not an easy task. They had no capital, no defence force and did not inherit a central government. Moreover, many areas were in shambles after the riots and the mass migrations. The economy was left completely shattered.

Jinnah dexterously tackled all the problems and also ensured that the law and order was maintained at all costs. He moved to Lahore to supervise the refugee problem. He settled many controversial issues but as fate would have it, he did not get as much time as was needed. He breathed his last on 11 September 1948. Due to his contribution towards the country, Pakistan continues to revere him as a leader who got them their homeland against all odds.

DID YOU KNOW?

- Jinnah had a high sense of fashion. He had over 200 suits and never wore the same tie twice.
- He was called Quaid-e-Azam, which means 'the great leader'.
- Jinnah married a Parsi woman after his first wife passed away within weeks of their marriage.

MUSTAFA KEMAL ATATÜRK

Mustafa Kemal Atatürk was a brave and daring national hero of Turkey. He is rightly hailed as the father of modern Turkey, the key player behind the formation of the republic.

EARLY LIFE

Mustafa was born in 1881 in the then Ottoman Empire. As a child, he was sent to the military academy in Istanbul. He was a meritorious student and his mathematics teacher was so impressed by him that he gave him the title 'Kemal'.

EARLY CAREER

Mustafa had a strong military background. He held a number of posts in the Ottoman Army from 1909 to 1918. In World War I, he was the commander of the 19th division. When the war was over, the sultan, Abdul Hamid II, saw that they had to either accept British or American supremacy.

However, Mustafa believed that Turkey should be independent and should be a republic as well. He not only denied the acceptance of any foreign rule but also of a monarch. He was hailed as the 'Father of Turkey', hence given the title 'Atatürk'.

ESTABLISHMENT OF THE REPUBLIC OF TURKEY

In 1919, Atatürk fought the advances of the Allied forces and ensured the safety of Turkey from external invasion. Atatürk had to engage in a number of battles with Greece and Armenia before being able to declare Turkey's complete independence on 29 October 1923.

PRESIDENT OF TURKEY

Mustafa Kemal Atatürk was the obvious choice to lead the young nation because of the valour he exhibited in securing the liberty of

Turkey. Moreover, he raised his voice against the despotism of the Sultan and earned the trust and respect of the people.

As president, he ensured a radical turnover of how the country was run earlier. He included reformism, nationalism, secularism, populism, republicanism and statism—now known as the six arrows of Kamalism, which means the ideologies upon which the new government rested. These proved to be the pillars on which Turkey stood.

He wanted to break the radical customs of the Ottoman Empire by including western and liberal culture. He also wanted to establish the Turkish language as he knew that language played a vital role in strengthening the roots of any country.

REFORMS

Atatürk encouraged all Turks to wear modern European clothing instead of the traditional ones. He wanted Turkey to be different from the other Islamic societies and the way one dressed was an important factor in that direction. He was even ready to employ force if need be. The Islamic calendar was replaced with the western one in 1925. Three years later, he took the major step of introducing the international numeric system.

Atatürk left no stone unturned in creating a unique identity for the Turkish. He even presented the new Turkish alphabet to replace the Arabic script. Atatürk aimed at separating religion and government. He had to start from the basic level and with this aim, he focused to modernize the classical local village education. The Law of Unification of Education was passed in 1924 which brought a uniformity of education imparted to all in the country.

Atatürk changed the country from being ruled on the basis of theocracy to a secular modern republic. He separated Islamic law from state law. He also introduced the Hat Law in 1925, urging the people to wear European hats instead of their traditional headgear.

Atatürk sought to include more women into political and social life. He wanted Turkish women to dress, receive education and pursue their dreams as any other woman of a civilized nation. To destroy class distinction, he passed the Civil Code which ensured that women were equal to men.

Turkey is today ahead of its time owing to the farsightedness of Atatürk. Atatürk died of liver cirrhosis in 1938. His statues are found all over Turkey to acknowledge his contribution.

DID YOU KNOW?

- Atatürk never fathered any children but adopted twelve girls and one boy.
- He wrote a geometry book in which he named geometrical terms in Turkish language.
- There is a flower called 'Atatürk' named after him.

NARENDRA MODI

Narendra Modi, the Indian prime minister, is a charismatic personality. His meteoric rise, from a tea-seller to the prime minister of India, is awe-inspiring.

EARLY LIFE

Narendra Modi was born into a very humble family on 17 September 1950 in the small town of Vadnagar, Gujarat. His parents were Damodardas Mulchand Modi and Heeraben Modi. To help his father meet the needs of the family, Modi started selling tea at Vadnagar railway station and later even opened a tea stall.

Modi exhibited oratorial and theatrical skills right from his childhood. He was equally interested in games and sports and displayed an immense love for his country always. He left home after school and travelled across the country understanding its diversity and culture.

ENTERING POLITICS

Narendra Modi joined the RSS in 1971. He worked tirelessly for the organization, waking up at 5 a.m. every morning. In 1975, when emergency was declared in India, bans were imposed on organizations like the RSS. This angered Modi and he went around in disguise distributing pamphlets opposing the government. His skills as a leader couldn't remain unnoticed, and Modi joined the Bharatiya Janata Party in 1985. His remarkable management skills during L.K. Advani's Rath Yatra were appreciated and his stature in the party grew. Finally, when the BJP won the Gujarat Assembly election in 1995, Keshubhai Patel was made the chief minister with Modi occupying a responsible position in the cabinet.

CHIEF MINISTER

Narendra Modi took over the responsibility of the chief minister of Gujarat in 2001 owing to the failing health of Keshubhai Patel. Since then, the manner in which he governed Gujarat has become exemplary. Some of his achievements as the chief minister included electrification of all villages, growth in tourism and solving the water crisis. Gujarat boasts of having the largest solar panel in Asia.

PRIME MINISTER

Considering his potential, he was declared as a prime ministerial candidate for the 2014 Lok Sabha elections. During his campaign, he went out to the masses and convinced them of a better tomorrow. The BJP witnessed a historic victory by winning 282 seats out of 534. After a resounding victory in the Lok Sabha elections 2019, with 303 seats secured by the BJP alone (NDA won 350 seats), the prime minister is now serving a glorious second term.

BUILDING INDIA

Modi brought in a fresh wave of change to Indian politics. He is a progressive leader, teeming with ideas about growth. To make India self-reliant in industrial production, he started the 'Make in India' campaign.

Swachh Bharat Abhiyan, launched on 2 October 2014, was a masterstroke in improving the image of India. To bring in fresh ideas and thoughts, Modi replaced the Planning Commission with National Institution for Transforming India (NITI) Aayog whose main objective was to find different ways of developing India on all fronts.

Making each person economically stable has been a dream of the Indian government under Modi. He started the Jan Dhan Yojna, urging every Indian to open a bank account. Facilities like credit, insurance and pension are provided to all account holders.

Modi also planned hundred smart cities and the Clean Ganga Mission. With an objective of improving foreign relations, Modi has visited many countries and assured them of full assistance from

India in case of investment. Modi has also initiated the project of constructing ten crore public toilets by 2019.

PERSONA

Narendra Modi is trying to reach out to each individual of India. 'Development for All' is his mantra and with this objective in mind, he took strong steps of demonetization and implemented the Goods and Service Tax (GST). These steps to curb corruption will surely take India to opulence and glory.

DID YOU KNOW?

- Narendra Modi is a brand–conscious person and buys his clothes only from the brand named 'Jade Blue'.
- Modi wanted to be a monk at Ramakrishna Mission and didn't have any intention of joining politics.
- He is a pure vegetarian and does yoga to stay fit.

NELSON MANDELA

Think of South Africa and the one name that reverberates in our minds is that of Nelson Mandela. He was fondly called Madiba by his people after the clan to which he belonged.

EARLY LIFE

Born in the small village of Mvezo, Transkei, on 18 July 1918, Rolihlahla Mandela was fed by stories of valour of his ancestors, right from his early childhood. His parents were Nonqaphi Nosekeni and Nkosi Mphakanyiswa Gadla Mandela, principal counsellor to the acting king of the Thembu people, Jongintaba Dalindyebo. In 1930, when he was only twelve years old, his father passed away and he became a ward of Jongintaba at the great palace in Mqhekezweni.

Mandela began his formal education. He started going to primary school in Qunu where his teacher, Miss Mdingane, gave him the name Nelson in accordance with the custom of giving all schoolchildren 'Christian' names. He completed his junior certificate at Clarkebury Boarding Institute and went on to Healdtown, a Wesleyan secondary school of some repute, where he matriculated.

MADIBA'S STRUGGLE

Madiba enrolled himself in the law college at the University of Witwatersrand where he faced racism. Appalled by the indignities faced by blacks, he joined the African National Congress (ANC) in 1943 to fight against colonialism and imperialism. He initiated many protests and guerrilla wars against the British and was arrested in 1964. He had to face imprisonment for twenty-seven years due to his demand for freedom.

Mandela was finally released on 11 February 1990. On 26 April 1994, more than twenty-two million South Africans turned out to cast ballots in the country's first multiracial parliamentary elections in history. On 10 May, Mandela was sworn in as the first black president of South Africa after an overwhelming majority chose the African National Congress (ANC) to lead the country, with Frederik de Klerk serving as his first deputy.

MADIBA AS ADMINISTRATOR

Madiba encouraged tolerance and forgiveness, and was a champion for the cause of peace. He wanted to establish a government wherein human rights were given supreme importance and the police would guard the honour and dignity of every individual. He formed a multiracial 'Government of National Unity'.

He also gave a new meaning to activism by fearlessly standing up against domination by both the whites and the blacks. He led by example by including South Africa's political and racial rivals in nation-building.

LAYING DOWN OF CONSTITUTION

Madiba laid a new constitution for South Africa in 1996 which helped establish a strong central government, based on the ideals of equality of races and development.

Mandela's primary agenda was the removal of poverty, maintaining law and order and proper distribution of wealth. By 1999, South Africa was galloping towards progress.

PHILANTHROPIST MADIBA

After retiring from politics in 1999, he devoted himself to the cause of humanity. He established several organizations to aid social service, including The Nelson Mandela Foundation and The Elders. This was the time when he addressed the grave issue of HIV/AIDS which was earlier overlooked. He was also involved in peace negotiations of other African countries. Mandela passed away on 5 December 2013 from a recurrent lung function, leaving behind a void that can never be filled.

DID YOU KNOW?

- Over a period of forty years, Mandela received 260 awards, including the prestigious Nobel Peace Prize which he received jointly with de Klerk in 1993.
- In 2009, the UN declared his birthday, 18 July, as the 'Nelson Mandela International Day'.
- The poem 'Invictus' by William Ernest Henley gave inspiration to Mandela while he was in prison.

OPRAH WINFREY

Oprah Winfrey really epitomizes the 'win' in her surname as she won against all odds where others would have given up. Her struggles have taken her to an acme of success and she is rightfully considered the 'Queen of Media'.

EARLY LIFE

Oprah Winfrey was born on 29 January 1954 in Kosciusko, Mississippi. She was born into poverty to an unwed mother. Her maternal grandmother brought her up till she was six years old. She got her lessons of the Bible from her grandmother. Even at such a tender age, Oprah was an impressive speaker and earned herself the name 'The Preacher'. Her favourite pastime was to interview her corncob dolls and the crows sitting on the fence.

Oprah was sent to her mother owing to financial crisis of her grandmother. Since her mother used to stay out for a long time due to her work, Oprah was lonely, and later became a victim of sexual abuse.

She ran away from her house at the age of thirteen. The pain and indignation she had endured all these years shook her to the core.

ENTERING HIGH SCHOOL

Her mother found Oprah and enrolled her in a high school. But Oprah felt insecure amidst the students from well-to-do families and started stealing money from home. Her mother sent her to her stepfather, who taught her discipline, and soon Oprah was counted among the brilliant students of her class. Her oratory and dramatic skills were acknowledged in school as well.

EARLY CAREER

In her last years of schooling, a local radio station gave Oprah the offer of reading the news which kickstarted her career in public speaking. But she did not give up her studies, and even won a scholarship to Tennessee University. During this time, she also won two beauty pageant awards. Soon she got an offer from Baltimore, Maryland TV channel to be a news reader and she joined it without completing her graduation. But she lost this job as she was too emotive for a news reader.

When Oprah was disillusioned about her life, a new road opened up for her. She got the offer to host a television talk show, 'People are Talking'. After hosting the show for seven years, Oprah became a renowned name in the television industry.

IMMENSE POPULARITY

Oprah moved to Chicago in 1984 to host a morning talk show—A.M. Chicago. Thanks to her talent, the low-rated show became the no. 1 talk show in television and was later called *The Oprah Winfrey Show*. Broadcasted for almost two decades, it has been the most talked-about show in the US. She has also founded her own production company, Harpo, Inc.

LIVING LEGACY

Oprah is a highly successful woman and believes in making her contribution towards the society. The setting up of the Oprah Winfrey Leadership Academy in Johannesburg for girls is a step towards this. *Time* magazine has named her as one of the most influential people in the world.

Despite Oprah's tremendous success, she humorously quips that she has her feet firmly planted on the ground; it's just that she wears good quality shoes.

DID YOU KNOW?

- Oprah is the first black woman billionaire and the richest African-American.
- President Barack Obama awarded the highest civilian award, the Presidential Medal of Freedom, to Oprah.
- Her original name was Orpah, after a Biblical character. But, since people couldn't pronounce her name, they called her Oprah.

P.V. NARASIMHA RAO

P.V. Narasimha Rao has been called the Chanakya of modern India and the Father of Indian Economic Reforms. He was the 10th prime minister of India.

EARLY LIFE

P.V. Narasimha Rao was born on 28 June 1921 to Ranga Rao and Rukminamma in Vangara village of Karimnagar district in Andhra Pradesh. He was born in a modest agrarian family. Before moving to politics, he, along with one of his cousins, edited a Telugu magazine called *Kakatiya Patrika*. They also used to write articles under the pen name Jaya-Vijaya.

POLITICAL CAREER

P.V. Narasimha Rao was a freedom fighter during the Indian independence struggle. He served in the Andhra Cabinet and later became the chief minister from 1971 to 1973. His tenure was much appreciated for the land reforms that he initiated. He was a very efficient man and therefore went on to serve several diverse portfolios like home affairs, defence and foreign affairs during the prime ministerships of Indira Gandhi and Rajiv Gandhi.

He was on the verge of giving up politics but the assassination of Rajiv Gandhi, the then Congress president, made it necessary for him to take over the reins of the party, and after the election, the country as well. He won his seat from Nandyal by a whopping margin of more than five lakh votes. He broke many norms after he took over as the prime minister—he appointed Manmohan Singh, who was a non-political person, as the finance minister; Subramanian Swamy, who was in the opposition, was appointed as the chairman of the commission on labour standards and international trade; Atal Bihari Vajpayee, who was the leader of the opposition, was sent to the UN meeting to represent India.

NARASIMHA RAO AS THE PRIME MINISTER

Rao's economic reforms were a milestone in the progress of India. He made a paradigm shift from mixed economic model to a market-driven one. To meet the economic crisis of 1991, he opened up to foreign investments.

He also gave impetus to national nuclear security, energized the Indian Army and wiped out terrorism from Punjab.

Rao established diplomatic relations with many countries of Western Europe, China and the US. He allowed Israel to build an embassy in India. These strategic movements made him draw the attention of the international community towards the involvement of Pakistan in terrorism in India. The Bombay (now Mumbai) bombings on 12 March 1993 were a crisis situation for the entire country but he managed the catastrophe well.

MEETING CHALLENGES

Narasimha Rao has earned the rare distinction of being the only democratic leader in the free world who managed to liberate the Indian economy despite having a minority government. Because of this achievement, Rao has been hailed as a reformer who stood out amongst some of the world's greatest leaders like Margaret Thatcher, Ronald Reagan and Franklin D. Roosevelt. Rao steered the country out of an almost bankruptcy-like situation by bringing in liberalization. It was his government that brought in the TADA (Terrorist and Disruptive Activities [Prevention] Act) and directed the army to stop foreign infiltrators.

The Latur earthquake in 1993 was a major mishap but his relief operations, using modern technology, were remarkable and have been praised by many.

DEATH AND LEGACY

On 23 December 2004, Narasimha Rao suffered a major heart attack and passed away at the age of eighty-three.

The scope of the economic liberalization that he ushered in India makes him stand out as one of the best prime ministers that India has ever had since independence.

DID YOU KNOW?

- Future prime ministers, Atal Bihari Vajpayee and Manmohan Singh, continued the economic reform policies pioneered by Rao's government, and achieved success.
- He was so smitten by technological advancement that he used to spend hours learning about web designing, programming, etc.
- Rao was able to speak sixteen languages, which included Oriya, Bengali, Marathi, Hindi, Tamil, Urdu and a few foreign languages like French, Spanish and German.

PAUL KEATING

As an astute politician, Paul Keating is considered by many as one of the finest prime ministers of Australia.

EARLY LIFE

Keating was born in Sydney, on 18 January 1944. His father was a boilermaker for the New South Wales Government Railways. Keating grew up in a modest working-class suburb in western Sydney. He was very close to his mother as well as his grandmother and often said that it was the love of these two women that gave him a lot of strength later in life.

Keating inherited his interest in politics from his father who was also a leading local Labour Party member. Keating left school at fourteen and worked as a clerk at the Sydney Country Council, the electrical distributor of Sydney. Later, he left this job to become a research assistant for a trade union. Around this time, Keating also joined the Labour Party. In 1966, he became the president of the New South Wales Youth Council.

POLITICAL CAREER

In 1969, when Keating was twenty-five years old, he was elected to the House of Representatives. In the government, Keating mostly remained inactive and was a backbencher. In December 1975, the Labour Party was defeated in the elections and Keating occupied the front bench in the opposition. There, he emerged as an aggressive debater.

In 1981, Keating was elected as the president of the New South Wales Labour Party. In 1983, he became the treasurer of Australia and he made extensive tax reforms, and the Australian economy blossomed.

PREMIER

Keating was sworn in as the 24th prime minister of Australia in 1991. The measures which Keating had taken as the treasurer were taken up in full gusto by him. Australia was going through unemployment and he sought to address it. The National Training Authority was established to redress the low national savings and labour market. He also took steps to recognize the rights of indigenous people.

FOREIGN RELATIONS

Throughout his premiership, Keating took a number of steps to maintain close ties with the neighbouring countries. He often said that no country in the world was more important to Australia than Indonesia. Keating initiated the Asia-Pacific Economic Cooperation (APEC) wherein he encouraged an annual meet of the leaders. Keating pursued improved and harmonious relations with countries of Asia, particularly Indo-China.

FORMING A REPUBLIC

Keating firmly believed that Australia should be a republic and thus proposed to reform the constitution so that Australia could become one. However, the referendum was not successful, but the present government is of the opinion that it would consider declaring Australia a republic after the completion of the reign of Elizabeth II.

RESIGNATION

Following the defeat of the Australian Labour Party in March 1996, Keating resigned from the parliament. But he is still associated with public life and takes interest in national issues.

DID YOU KNOW?

- Keating's political hero was Winston Churchill.
- Altohugh he did not receive any formal education after the age of fourteen, today he is a visiting faculty to universities across the world.

POPE FRANCIS

Pope Francis is a symbol of hope and change in the Vatican. Breaking away from the extravagant lifestyle of the clergy, he has earned respect across the world for his simplicity.

EARLY LIFE

Jorge Mario Bergoglio was born on 17 December 1936 in Buenos Aires, Argentina. His parents were Italian immigrants and had a modest life. The young boy loved soccer, and spending time with friends. He entered the novitiate in the Society of Jesus after graduating from a technical school as a chemical technician. Bergoglio was influenced by his grandmother and got his first lessons of religion from her.

RECOGNIZING HIS CALLING

Bergoglio experienced the seeds of a religious vocation while the seventeen-year-old went for confession. Afterwards, he heard a voice which convinced him that he should become a priest.

PRIESTHOOD

Bergoglio was ordained as a priest in 1969 and he began serving as a Jesuit provincial of Argentina in 1973. He spent more than fifteen years in his formation wherein he continued to take spiritual training as a Jesuit, and during this time he witnessed the tumultuous politics of Argentina. He continued with his service of comforting the sufferer. After almost four decades of entering the seminary, Archbishop Bergoglio was elevated to a cardinal by Pope John Paul II at St Peter's Square.

CONTRIBUTION AS A CARDINAL

Bergoglio consistently stood for all the catholic values and therefore was appalled at any sort of atrocity. He cared for the social situation of the needy, the elderly and the children. Voicing his protest against the injustices meted out by the privileged class, he was often criticized for having political aspirations. However, such is not the case. As a spiritual leader, he felt a responsibility towards the proper guidance of his people. He pleaded to people, especially those who hid behind the bubble of abundance, to realize their social responsibility. The best thing about him was, and still is, his ability to forgive, a quality which marks him above ordinary mortals. In 1986, Father Bergoglio travelled to Germany to advance his theological studies. Upon his return to Argentina, he was sent to Cordova where he served as confessor and a spiritual director. Nobody anticipated that he would rise to the position of Pope someday.

BECOMING THE POPE

Cardinal Berogilo's influence extended even beyond Buenos Aires. When Pope Benedict VI visited Brazil, Bergoglio was chosen to write a confidential document on the church despite the presence of many other senior priests. On 13 March 2013, he was named as the 266th Pope of the Roman Catholic Church. He was the first non-European and first Jesuit priest to become the Pope. The people of Latin America, and his country Argentina, were overjoyed when he was named the Pope.

DID YOU KNOW?

- As a true Argentine, Pope Francis is a big fan of the tango.
- It is said that he pays his own bills and does not send an assistant to do so.
- Pope Francis is a linguist and is able to speak in Spanish, Italian, Latin, English, German, Ukrainian, French and Portuguese.

PUSHPA KAMAL DAHAL

The life of Pushpa Kamal Dahal, popularly known as Prachanda Dahal, is a journey from bullet to ballot, from insurgency to politics. He is the man behind establishing democracy in Nepal.

EARLY LIFE
Pushpa Kamal Dahal was born on 11 December 1954 in a small village of Nepal in a humble family of farmers. Pushpa Kamal had a lot of interest in studies, and despite various difficulties, he never gave up.

ENTRY INTO POLITICS
Pushpa Kamal was drawn towards communist ideas. He headed the All Nepal National Free Students' Union and believed that it was only through arms that a nation could be changed. It is during his insurgency days that he named himself 'Prachanda', which meant 'Fierce'.

Influenced by Mao Zedong of China and the ideology of a classless state, he founded the Communist Party of Nepal (Maoist) in March 1995.

FROM INSURGENCY TO PEACE
On 13 February 1996, Prachanda declared an insurgency campaign to abolish monarchy in Nepal. The war continued for ten long years and he remained underground for many years. This revolution laid the foundation of a modern Nepal.

Those in power realized that the people were not happy with their governance. The revolution spread a wave of political consciousness among the people. Prachanda became the spokesperson for all marginalized people. However, gradually, he felt that insurgency would not be able to give people their rights as much as peace would do.

With the wave of globalization, Prachanda realized that to ensure rapid growth and development of the nation, establishing peace within the country as well as with the outside world was essential.

He also understood that with able leadership, Nepal can reach to great heights of success. He made his first public appearance in June 2006 to negotiate the creation of the country's new government.

The turning point was the signing of the Comprehensive Peace Agreement in November 2006 and he and his rebels laid down their arms in 2008.

PRIME MINISTER

Although Prachanda was sworn in as the prime minister of democratic Nepal on 15 August 2008, he had to resign in 2009 due to power struggles. He came back to power in 2016 and tried to establish friendly relations with neighbouring countries like India and China. When he was elected as the prime minister for the first time, he himself admitted that he found it very difficult to understand the complexities of party politics. But he was more confident when he came to power the second time. He tried to resolve the problem of national consensus among parties to come to a common understanding. He also laid particular emphasis on the growth of tourism.

DID YOU KNOW?

- Dahal had overthrown a 240-year-old feudal monarchy.
- He holds the Indian prime minister, Narendra Modi, in high regard and considers him as a great inspiration in his life.
- He was named Pushpa Kamal by his teacher, which means 'Lotus Flower' because of his mild behaviour.

RAMON MAGSAYSAY

Ramon Magsaysay, the seventh president of the Philippines, was the champion of the people. He was an outstanding crusader of democracy and the idol of the masses.

EARLY LIFE

Ramon del Fierro Magsaysay was of mixed race ancestry and was born in Iba, Zambales, on 31 August 1907 to a poor family. His father Exequiel Magsaysay was a blacksmith and his mother Perfecta del Fiero a schoolteacher. Magsaysay earned a bachelor's degree in commerce. In college, he worked as a chauffeur and an automobile mechanic to support himself.

WORLD WAR II

When World War II broke out, Magsaysay joined the 31st Infantry Division of the Philippine Army. When the US surrendered Bataan, a province in the Central Luzon region of Philippines, to Japan in 1942, Magsaysay fled to the hills. He narrowly escaped arrest by the Japanese on about four occasions. In the hills, Magsaysay organized the Western Luzon Guerrilla Forces and became its captain.

Thereafter, for about three years, Magsaysay functioned under Colonel Merrill's famed guerrilla outfit. Magsaysay was instrumental in getting the Zambales coast cleared of the Japanese troops. On 29 January 1945, the American forces landed in the Zambales coast along with the Philippine Commonwealth troops.

Magsaysay had also been instrumental in crushing the Hukbalahap uprising of the peasants against the government through administrative reforms, but realized that the root cause of such an uprising was people's dissatisfaction, which had to be addressed first.

ENTERING POLITICS

Magsaysay joined politics after being elected as the representative of Zambales in 1946. He was made the chairman of the National Defense Committee. In this regard, Magsaysay travelled to the US for obtaining additional benefits for the Filipino veterans and also for getting military assistance.

He applied guerrilla efforts he learnt during World War II against the formation of the Filipino Army. He also sent a positive message about the government across to the people.

PRESIDENCY

Ramon Magsaysay had grown in popularity and thus the Nacionalista Party supported him for presidency against the incumbent Elpidio Quirino in 1953. Ramon was against communism and desired to oust it from Asia. With this aim, he formed the Manila Pact of 1954 that aimed to demolish Communist-Marxist movements in Asia.

CONTRIBUTION

Magsaysay ushered in a new era of growth and development in Philippines along with restoration of the trust of the people. He created the Presidential Complaints and Action Committee which boosted the trust of the people towards the working of the government.

Magsaysay allocated land to ordinary farmers and also provided financial assistance to the rural people. Filipinos still sing praises of this enterprising man for providing assistance in building wells. Vast irrigation projects and power plants were also set up. In short, Magsaysay gave voice to the hitherto voiceless people.

Magsaysay established friendly relations with Japan and helped to fight the spread of communism.

DEATH AND LEGACY

Magsaysay met with his sad demise on 17 March 1957 by a plane crash. His death came as a shock to the nation. The Ramon Magsaysay award was established in 1957, in honour of the president, and is awarded to those who are examples of integrity and selfless service to people.

DID YOU KNOW?

- Magsaysay started the practice of framing campaign jingles in the Philippines.
- The 'Barong Tagalog', the traditional dress of the Philippines, was popularized as formal wear by Magsaysay.
- Magsaysay was truly a man of the people and thus opened the gates of Malacanang (the official residence and workplace of the president) to them.

RECEP TAYYIP ERDOĞAN

Prime Minister Recep Tayyip Erdoğan is undoubtedly the most powerful Turkish political leader. Interestingly, he is also an environmentalist and a champion of great infrastructure.

EARLY LIFE

Recep Tayyip Erdoğan was born in February 26, 1954 in Istanbul, Turkey. He had a very humble upbringing. His early childhood was spent in Rize where his father worked as the coast guard. Later, they moved back to Istanbul when he was a teenager. He attended the religious Imam Hatip School.

ENTRY INTO POLITICS

Erdoğan played an active role in politics since his college days. However, in 1980, due to a military coup, all political parties were dissolved. Martial law was declared in Turkey till the new constitution came into action. Erdoğan felt restless during this time as he could not express himself freely.

The National Salvation Party regrouped itself as the New Welfare Party in 1983. Erdoğan found his calling and joined the party. He was a dedicated worker, and in 1989, he rose to the position of the head of the Istanbul City branch. He toiled day and night for the party and was awarded with success in the municipal elections held in 1989.

In 1994, Erdoğan was elected as the mayor of Istanbul. He soon banned alcohol from public places and turned his attention to pressing issues like water shortage, pollution and infrastructure of not only Istanbul but also the country.

NEW BEGINNING

Erdoğan founded the Justice and Development Party (AKP) in

2001. The year 2002 marked the glorious victory of AKP in the parliamentary elections. He was elected as the prime minister of Turkey on 9 March 2003. His prime focus then was to improve the economic conditions of Turkey. Inflation was at its highest and so he invited foreign investments which led to the rise in the per capita income of the people. He also signed a treaty with a Russian company to build a nuclear facility in Turkey.

PRESIDENT OF TURKEY

After Erdoğan served as the prime minister for three successive terms quite successfully, he was the obvious choice to run the elections for the president of Turkey. He assumed office on 28 August 2014. He is the first Turkish president to be elected directly. Although the post had been a ceremonial one at the beginning, but gradually he incorporated more powers to the post. His government prioritized education and increased its budget manifold. He also started the concept of 'green card' for the poor to provide them health benefits. Emphasis was laid on improving public transport, especially railways. The country has grown immensely and has made a mark for itself in the world stage since he has assumed power. The president also managed to keep the inflation at bay even when the whole world was reeling under its massive force.

SECULAR TURKEY

Turkey is not a radical nation; secularism is one of its strong pillars. Erdoğan feels that the Turks should be given the opportunity to practise Islam if they want. Erdoğan seeks to continue the legacy of extending friendship to all nations and living peacefully without compromising on dignity. He has played a major role in modernizing the country.

DID YOU KNOW?

- Erdoğan used to sell bread and lemonade as a teenager to earn extra money.
- He banned the use of social media sites like Twitter and Facebook as it gave rise to chaos in society.
- He was listed as one of the '100 Most Influential People' by *Time* magazine in 2004.

ROBERT MUGABE

Robert Mugabe was the most significant political actor of Zimbabwe for four decades till his forced retirement in 2017. He led the country from being a British colony to an independent nation.

EARLY LIFE

Robert Gabriel Mugabe was born on 21 February 1924 in Kutama, Southern Rhodesia (now Zimbabwe). Robert's father was a carpenter who worked at a Jesuit mission in South Africa. His mother was a teacher.

Mugabe was schooled at the local Jesuit mission under the school director Father O'Hea who left a very powerful influence on the boy. His values resonated so strongly with Mugabe that he went on to become a teacher himself.

Mugabe got a bachelor's degree in history and English from the University of Fort Hare. He then returned to his hometown.

By 1955, Mugabe moved to Northern Rhodesia and taught for four years in a training college while simultaneously pursuing a correspondence course for his Bachelor of Administration. Thereafter, he moved to Ghana where he began his political activities as a Marxist.

ENTERING POLITICS

In 1960, when Mugabe returned to his hometown in Southern Rhodesia, he encountered a transformed environment. The new colonial government had displaced tens of thousands of black families. The government also defied the black majority rule which led to violent protests.

In July 1960, he addressed a crowd of 7,000 people in the heart of Harare, gathered to protest the arrest of black leaders. Mugabe braved police threats and told them how Ghana had successfully used Marxism to achieve independence.

Within weeks, Mugabe was elected as the public secretary of the National Democratic Party. Mugabe borrowed the political model from Ghana and swiftly consolidated a militant youth league. This league began spreading ways to achieve black independence in Rhodesia but the government banned the National Democratic Party at the end of 1961. The supporters of the party then formed a movement—the Zimbabwe African People's Union (ZAPU)—which grew to include around 4,50,000 members.

In April 1961, Mugabe had publicly announced his willingness to start a guerrilla war.

THE FORMATION OF THE ZANU

In 1963, Mugabe formed a resistance movement which was called the Zimbabwe African National Union (ZANU). The same year Mugabe was arrested in Southern Rhodesia and sent to prison for over a decade.

In 1974, Ian Smith, the then Southern Rhodhesian colonial governor, allowed Mugabe to leave prison and attend a conference in Lusaka, Zambia. It was Smith's attempt to consider majority rule. Since Mugabe sensed that he was being used to stall the transfer of power, he seized the opportunity and fled to Southern Rhodesia and assembled a troop of Rhodesian guerrilla trainees, whom he used to begin a battle that went on throughout the 1970s.

The British rulers agreed to support changeover to black majority rule. Southern Rhodesia was liberated from British rule in 1980 and it became the independent Republic of Zimbabwe. Mugabe was elected as the prime minister of the new republic.

MUGABE'S PRESIDENCY

In just about a week after the union of the ZANU and ZAPU, Mugabe was appointed as the president of Zimbabwe in 1987. The first major task that Mugabe undertook as the president was to contain the country's failing economy.

In 1989, Mugabe implemented a five-year plan, and by 1994, the economy saw positive growth in farming, mining and manufacturing sectors. Mugabe also built clinics and schools in Zimbabwe during this time.

THE MILITARY TAKEOVER

Mugabe refused to give up power despite the fact that there was growing resentment in the party regarding the share of power. In November 2017, after Mugabe dismissed vice president Emmerson Mnangagwa, the military became active and moved tanks to the capital, Harare. He claims that he is a victim of a military coup. Mugabe decided to transfer power on 22 November 2017. His tenure of thirty-seven years was applauded by everyone in the country.

DID YOU KNOW?

- Mugabe's middle name Gabriel has been taken from the Bible where the angel Gabriel is the messenger of God who imparts His wisdom.
- He won a lottery ticket of 1,00,000 Zimbabwean dollars in 2000.
- Mugabe earned two law degrees while he was behind bars.

RONALD REAGAN

R onald Reagan was the 40th president of the US. He brought back the 'roar' of the US by restoring its past glory, by infusing his countrymen with enthusiasm.

EARLY LIFE

Ronald Reagan was born on 6 February 1911 to Nelle Clyde and John Edward Jack Reagan in Tempico, Illinois. Young Reagan moved from city to city as his father was a struggling shoe salesman. He was a self-reliant boy and had great faith in God. Having completed his school education, he got scholarship to Eureka College to study economics and sociology. He excelled in sports, theatre, swimming and student politics.

DABBLING VARIED JOBS

After graduating, Reagan took up the job of a radio announcer at various radio stations. In 1937, he signed a contract with the Warner Brothers and began his career in Hollywood which lasted for three long decades.

Meanwhile, he also enrolled in the Army Enlisted Reserve in 1937 and served in various positions till 1943. After his return, he joined motion pictures and also worked in television. He hosted several shows on television and it was while working there that he thought of entering politics.

ENTERING POLITICS

Reagan explicitly supported republicans. He ran for the post of governor of California in 1966 and won by a margin of almost one million votes. He served his second term in 1970. He was quite successful as a governor and brought in many changes in taxation and protection of the environment.

He was sworn in as the president in 1981 at the age of seventy. He stated in his inaugural speech that the government should be the 'problem solver' and not the 'problem'.

He hoped that the US would be a ray of light to all those nations that did not have freedom.

CONTRIBUTION AS THE PRESIDENT

When Reagan took over the office, inflation and unemployment were quite high. He brought in a number of changes and new policies in the social, domestic, economic and international arena to combat the dismal situation.

He increased the military budget and reduced spending in certain social programmes. He lowered tax rates, which eventually led to more investments, higher growth and even increase in wages. The US was gradually moving towards prosperity.

INTERNATIONAL RELATIONS

Reagan believed in achieving 'peace through strength'. He formulated a policy known as Reagan Doctrine through which he aimed at providing aid to nations fighting against communist governments. His main aim was to weaken Soviet-backed ideologies. This resulted in the Cold War between the US and the USSR. Even though he was spending a lot in strengthening the national defence, he still sought to improve relations with the Soviet Union.

Thus, he entered into an agreement with Mikhail Gorbachev wherein they decided to avoid intermediate range missile tests. His appeal to Gorbachev to 'tear down the wall' proved to be the turning point, which ended the Cold War. Reagan was vehemently against international terrorism and took strong steps to curb it. He sent forces to Libya as retaliation against attacking American soldiers.

SECOND INNINGS AS THE PRESIDENT

Ronald Reagan won a monumental victory against opponent Walter Mondale in the 1984 presidential elections. In his second presidential term, he vowed to fight against the drug menace and make schools and workplaces free from it.

First Lady Nancy Reagan founded the drug awareness programme called 'Just say no'.

DEATH AND LEGACY

Reagan announced through a letter that he was diagnosed with Alzheimer's disease in 1994. Good wishes and concern poured out for him. He left the office of the president in 1989 and moved to Bel Air in Los Angeles.

On 5 June 2004, this great public figure passed away. He died of pneumonia which was further complicated by Alzheimer's disease. A state funeral was conducted for him on 11 June.

DID YOU KNOW?

- Reagan saved around seventy-seven lives as a lifeguard.
- He became an FBI agent informing about communist sympathizers to the government.
- Reagan was a great storyteller and his jokes on the Russian-US relationship continue to be very popular even today.

ROSA PARKS

Rosa Parks has been called the mother of the American civil rights. She was an ordinary woman who could do extraordinary deeds; a woman of an indomitable spirit.

EARLY LIFE

Rosa Louise McCauley was born on 4 February 1913 to coloured parents in Tuskegee, Alabama. She grew up in the farm of her grandparents called Edward's Farm. Her parents were former slaves, and championed the cause of racial equality. She was exposed to racial discrimination quite early in life. As a child, she had to walk to school because the bus system was denied to coloured people. She later attended the State Teachers' High School but had to drop out soon as she had to take care of her ailing mother and grandmother. She earned her high school diploma after her marriage with Raymond Parks.

BIRTH OF A REBEL

Rosa joined the Montgomery chapter of the National Association for the Advancement of Coloured People and served as the chapter secretary. Little did Rosa realize that 1 December 1955 would go down into the pages of history because of her one act. While travelling in a bus, she refused to give up her seat to a white man on a Montgomery, Alabama bus and was arrested for this.

Rosa Parks became a role model for coloured people. She symbolized courage and ignited in others a desire to uphold their self-esteem. After Rosa was arrested, Edgar Daniel Nixon planned for a boycott of Montgomery's city buses. On the day of her trial, a large number of people gathered at Mt Zion Church in Montgomery to discuss further strategies, and they were led by none other than the iconic civil rights leader, Martin Luther King Jr. The Montgomery

Bus Boycott was a tremendous success and it lasted for 381 days.

On 5 December, Rosa was tried and found guilty of violating the law. She was fined $10 and $4 as court costs. But, by then, she had galvanized a great reform. She became the voice of the frustrated coloured people.

The Supreme Court decided on 13 November 1956 that racial segregation was unconstitutional. It was one of the most successful mass movements against racism in the whole world. She came to be known as the 'Mother of Civil Rights'.

HARDSHIPS

Even though Rosa Parks became a national figure, she was denied jobs everywhere because of her political leanings. Not only Rosa, but also her husband lost his job. She was harassed and even received life threats. Rosa was left with no choice but to leave Montgomery along with her husband and mother. She moved to Detroit, Michigan where she began a new chapter of her life.

ROSA AND HER MESSAGE

Rosa had always been inspired by her husband and she didn't want the spark of awakening among people to die. Rosa founded the Rosa and Raymond Parks Institute for Self-development. She wanted that the future generation should be aware of what went into securing freedom for people. She travelled across the US to extend her support to the cause of civil rights. In 1999, Rosa wrote that she chose to rebel because she was tired of giving in.

Time magazine designated her as one of the most influential people of the world in the 20th century. Her simple act of not giving up her seat changed history. She breathed her last on 24 October 2005.

DID YOU KNOW?

- To honour Rosa Parks, bus seats were left empty on the 50th anniversary of her arrest.
- Rosa differed in her opinion with Martin Luther King Jr as she believed in including more radical ways to fight against racism, unlike him who believed in completely peaceful ways.
- Her statue is the first African-American woman's to be placed at the Capitol's National Statutory Hall.

RUTH BADER GINSBURG

Ruth Bader Ginsburg has made her mark as a great strategist and lawyer. She is hailed as the architect of the modern women's movement.

EARLY LIFE
Ruth Joan Bader was born on 15 March 1933 in Brooklyn, New York. She belonged to a modest family and learnt the value of independence and education from her mother. The death of her mother was devastating for her and it left a void in her life.

TAKING UP LAW
Ruth Ginsburg showed great interest in law since she was a school student. She graduated from Cornell University with high honours in government. Later, she joined Harvard Law School. In the ruthless male-dominated world of law, she was often ridiculed and even sneered at for taking the places of capable men. Although she graduated at the top of her class, law firms refused to hire her because she was a woman.

Ginsburg excelled academically, eventually becoming the first female member of the prestigious Harvard Law Review. She was appointed as the first female faculty member in the law school's history. Ginsburg devoted a lot of her attention to women's rights. She successfully argued against a law which gave more housing and medical benefits to male members than women members of the armed forces. She fought not just those cases where women were the victims but believed that human rights of either gender should not be violated.

Having proven her mettle as a lawyer, Ginsburg was named a judge on the US Court of Appeals for the district of Columbia by President Jimmy Carter. She had the rare combination of political and intellectual skills and therefore Bill Clinton considered her the perfect person to deal with the conservatives. In 1993, she went on to become the 107th Supreme Court Justice.

ROLE IN JUDICIARY

Ginsburg was known for her calm and composed nature. She strongly advocated gender equality, rights of workers and the separation of the centre from the state. Her arguments were strong and vociferous. Ginsburg gave her landmark decision in 1996 in the 'US versus Virginia' case wherein she made it clear that the state-supported Virginia Military Institute could not refuse to admit women, as it was a case of gender discrimination. Her contributions to gender sensitivity bore fruit in 1999 when she won the American Bar Association's Thurgood Marshall Award for her contributions to gender equality. She stood up for civil rights as well.

HISTORIC DECISIONS

Ginsburg played a major role in passing Obamacare, which allowed Americans to access subsidies to healthcare. She was also instrumental in the decision of allowing same-sex marriage across all the fifty states of America.

In 1990, Ginsburg ruled that persons with mental disabilities have the right to live in the community rather than in institutions if medically and financially approved to do so.

Ginsburg is considered to be instrumental in passing the Lilly Ledbetter Fair Pay Act of 2009 which disallows any kind of discrimination of pay based on gender, race, age, religion, etc.

Expressing her liberal outlook, she has also participated in the #MeToo movement wherein she spoke about how she had to tackle the sexual advances of one of her professors. She has always maintained that she has never felt she was less for being a woman.

DID YOU KNOW?

- Ginsburg does twenty push-ups every day, followed by a 30-second plank.
- She was one of only nine women in a class of 500 at Harvard Law.
- Ginsburg regrets that she cannot sing, else she would have been in the opera.

SAM MANEKSHAW

Field Marshal Manekshaw is a figure in the history of the Indian Army who deserves our reverence. Known for his valour, he is rightly considered one of India's greatest generals.

EARLY LIFE

Sam was born to Parsi parents, Hormusji Manekshaw and Heerabai on 3 April 1914 in Amritsar, Punjab. His father was a doctor and therefore Sam also aspired to be a doctor. To accomplish his dream, he requested his father to send him to London to pursue a medical degree. Refused on the grounds that he was too young to go abroad, a rebellious Manekshaw took the entrance test of the Indian Military Academy (IMA) in Dehradun and was enrolled in 1932. After passing out in 1934, Manekshaw became the second lieutenant in the British Indian Army. Thus he started his glorious military career.

MILITARY CAREER

Sam Manekshaw was from the first batch of cadets of the IMA who got commissioned into the British Army. Thus, he is rightly termed as one of the Pioneers. His marvellous military career spanned over four decades.

Manekshaw led the 12 Frontier Force Regiment in Burma in 1942 and played a significant role during the Second World War. While fighting against the Japanese Army, he was hit by a machine gun firing. Yet, he fought and emerged victorious in this combat too. The British divisional commander was so impressed with his chivalry that he pinned his own Military Cross on Manekshaw's chest in the battlefield.

Manekshaw's popularity grew, and he was sent on difficult missions. Towards the end of World War II, he was sent to serve General Daisy in Indo-China. There he helped to repatriate over

10,000 prisoners of war, which was, indeed, a remarkable achievement.

POST-INDEPENDENCE

On 15 August 1947, Manekshaw was assigned the Gorkha Regiment and he came to be known as Sam Bahadur. He was later assigned the 16th Punjab Regiment because the 12th Regiment had gone to Pakistan after partition.

Manekshaw played a significant role in the Jammu-Kashmir Mission during 1947–48. Keeping in view his excellent military skills, he was made to command a division in Jammu and Kashmir. Sardar Vallabhbhai Patel included Manekshaw in the integration process of the country.

INDO-PAKISTAN WAR

The victory in the Indo-Pak war of 1965 was achieved under the leadership of Manekshaw. In 1969, Manekshaw became the chief of army staff.

In 1971, the problems related to East Pakistan were at a high. As a result of the atrocities of West Pakistan, the people from East Pakistan were escaping to India in large numbers. It became impertinent for India to go to war with Pakistan. Under Manekshaw's fine leadership, Pakistan was left with no choice but to surrender to India. He became a national hero and was decorated with the Padma Vibhushan in 1972.

FIELD MARSHAL

Manekshaw's retirement was postponed by six months in 1972. In 1973, the president of India honoured him with the title of field marshal. After two weeks, he resigned from active service but remained in the highest military position as a field marshal.

He passed away in 2008, leaving behind a legacy of discipline and hard work. The only religion he abided by throughout his life was the service to his nation.

DID YOU KNOW?

- Manekshaw wanted to be a gynaecologist.
- He participated in as many as five wars.
- He used to refer to Indira Gandhi as 'Sweetie' because of her Parsi connection; Feroze Gandhi was a Parsi.

SARDAR VALLABHBHAI PATEL

Sardar Vallabhbhai Patel was a man of few words but fast action. Without him, the concept of an integrated India would have been a dream. He is rightly called the 'Iron Man of India'.

EARLY LIFE

Vallabhai Patel was born in a small town of Gujarat, Nadiad on 31 October 1875. He belonged to an agricultural family. His father, Zaveribhai, had served in the army of the queen of Jhansi, and his mother, Ladbai, was a simple woman. At school, he emerged as a mischievous and witty boy who delighted his friends with his humour.

In 1913, at the age of thirty-five, Patel attained his law degree from England. He returned to India and started his practice in Godhra, Gujarat. He was an accomplished criminal lawyer and the British government offered him many posts, but he refused.

GANDHI AND HIS INFLUENCE

Sardar Patel shifted to Ahmedabad and joined the Indian National Congress after he attended one of Gandhiji's meetings. Patel led a No Tax Campaign against the British in Bardoli. Through his peaceful movement, he forced the government to return land to the farmers. Thus, he earned the title of 'Sardar', which means leader.

NATIONAL MOVEMENT

Sardar Patel joined Gandhiji and was drawn to his magnetic personality. He silently observed how Gandhi used to work, and they shared a thirty-year relationship. In 1930, he participated in the Salt Satyagraha movement led by Gandhiji, and even carried the baton of leadership when Gandhiji was imprisoned.

In 1932, Sardar Patel was elected as the president of the Indian National Congress. He started dreaming of a free and secular India.

The stage was set for the most decisive movement, namely, the Quit India Movement in 1942. All the major leaders like Gandhiji, Nehru and Sardar Patel were arrested and put behind bars in the Ahmednagar jail. He was sixty-eight years old, ill, but had a strong desire to do something for the nation. Sardar Patel became the home minister and the deputy prime minister after India's independence.

PATEL AND NATION-BUILDING

Achieving independence was a euphoric moment for India. However, the partition of India had cast a gloom over the entire nation. Sardar Patel, as the home minister, had to tackle the issue of mass partition. The other pressing issue was how to bring the princely states to India. The country's sovereignty was of supreme importance to Sardar Patel. He used persuasion, law and even force so that these states join the country.

Sardar Patel integrated a staggering number of 562 princely states into India. He was a true visionary and was a key force in establishing the Indian Administrative Service as well as the Indian Postal Service. Working on the various faces of nation-building, he realized the importance of having a strong defence, and thus not only expanded the army but also improved its infrastructure. Sardar Patel also dealt with the refugee issue and built several camps in Delhi, Punjab and West Bengal.

Sardar Patel passed away on 15 December 1950.

DID YOU KNOW?

- His birthday, 31 October, is celebrated as Rashtriya Ekta Diwas, as he was the one responsible for bringing more than 500 princely states together.
- While preparing for his law degree, he used to borrow books from his friends to study.
- During the non-cooperation movement, he travelled across the western part of India and recruited 3,00,000 members and collected 1.5 million rupees for the party fund.

SARVEPALLI RADHAKRISHNAN

An able statesman, a prolific scholar and a dynamic educationist, Dr Sarvepalli Radhakrishnan donned many more hats and was such a remarkable personality that Indians are still in awe of him.

EARLY LIFE

Sarvepalli Radhakrishnan was born on 5 December 1888 in Tiruttani in Tamil Nadu. He was brought up with a blend of Vedic knowledge, Hindu shastra and oriental teachings. This multi-religious exposure had a strong influence on his life and philosophy. He mastered both Indian and western philosophy; he graduated in European philosophy from Madras Christian College and wrote his thesis on Vedanta philosophy.

EARLY CAREER

Radhakrishnan began his teaching career in Madras Presidency College in 1909. In 1918, he moved to the University of Mysore as a professor. Radhakrishnan's writing transcended geographical and cultural boundaries. The West started paying attention to his philosophy with the help of his lectures. His Hibbert Lecture on the ideals of life led to the shaping of his famous book, *An Idealist View of Life*.

Radhakrishnan played different roles in Calcutta University, Andhra University and Benaras Hindu University (BHU). He represented Calcutta University at the congress of the Universities of the British empire. The years 1931 to 1936 saw him as the vice chancellor of Andhra University, and later, in 1939, he became the vice chancellor of BHU. His career bloomed as an academician and an educationist. He was a very popular teacher and his students looked up to him as a philosopher and guide.

In 1948, Radhakrishnan was made the chairman of the University

Education Commission and laid down the road map of university education for independent India. He recommended the setting up of a central University Grants Commission to maintain the standards of education in India. He also realized that education cannot be left to the centre, and state governments should also be given powers to decide on the matters of education.

ENTRY INTO POLITICS

After India attained her independence, the then prime minister, Pt Jawaharlal Nehru, was looking for people who had the capability to steer the country through difficult times. Dr Radhakrishnan was called to serve the country as a member of the executive board of UNESCO and as a member of the Constituent Assembly. Nehru also sent Dr Radhakrishnan as an ambassador to the Soviet Union. Stalin was highly impressed with his outlook and worldview.

Nehru and Dr Radhakrishnan's unwavering faith in democracy brought them together. In laying the foundation of a new India, Nehru, Gandhi and Radhakrishnan complemented one other. In 1952, Dr Radhakrishnan became the first vice president of India and, therefore, the first chairman of the Rajya Sabha. He served as the vice president for two terms before being elected as the second president of India in 1962.

During Radhakrishnan's presidential tenure, India witnessed strained relations with China and Pakistan. Despite two wars and the sad demise of two prime ministers, Dr Radhakrishnan ensured the smooth transition of power.

LEGACY

Dr Radhakrishnan not only acted as a bridge between Eastern and Western philosophy, he placed Indian philosophy on the world map. He blended philosophy with complex politics and taught the nation to uphold the spirit of the constitution.

DEATH

Dr Radhakrishnan passed away on 17 April 1975 and is still mourned as one of the finest intellectuals of independent India.

DID YOU KNOW?

- Since 1933, his name had been nominated for the Nobel Prize for Literature for five consecutive years, but he did not win it.
- While presiding over the Rajya Sabha sessions, he would start quoting lines from Sanskrit classics or the Bible to calm down the members.
- His birthday, 5 September, is celebrated as Teachers' Day in India.

SHEIKH HASINA

Sheikh Hasina Wazed, the prime minister of Bangladesh, is strong-willed and resolute. She is the leader of one of the world's most poverty-stricken countries.

EARLY LIFE

Sheikh Hasina is the daughter of the legendary Sheikh Mujibur Rehman, the first president of Bangladesh. She was born on 28 September 1947 in Bangladesh.

Sheikh Hasina saw her father go in and out of prison. She got her first lesson on politics from her parents. While studying at the University of Dhaka, she also worked for her father's party, as he was frequently imprisoned. Tragedy befell her on 15 August 1975 when, in a military coup, Sheikh Hasina lost her parents and three brothers and she was exiled for six years.

RETURN TO BANGLADESH

On her return in 1981, she took it upon herself to fulfil her father's vision of a 'Shonar Bangla' (Golden Bengal). She was elected to lead the Awami League Party and started voicing her opinions fearlessly. Although popular among the masses, she was not favoured by the ruling party and was put under house arrest. But Sheikh Hasina was ready to fight for establishing democracy.

POLITICAL CAREER

Bangladesh's first free general elections were held in 1991 after sixteen years and Sheikh Hasina became the leader of the opposition. Hasina kept up with her protests against the atrocities of the government.

Parliamentary elections were again held in 1996 and Sheikh Hasina became the prime minister of Bangladesh. It was not an easy task bringing order to a country facing corruption and poverty.

She was a dynamic leader and worked relentlessly to build the image of Bangladesh in the world domain.

MAJOR CONTRIBUTIONS

Sheikh has been elected as the leader of the people thrice, which proves the love and respect she enjoys. Under her leadership, power generation has increased, lighting up many villages and towns. She is constantly on the lookout for solutions to energy crises. The picture on the economic front is also brightening. The per capita income has increased, and it is expected that the curve would rise higher. She is toiling towards materializing Vision-21, which means turning Bangladesh into a digital Bangladesh.

Sheikh Hasina has earned tremendous respect in the world for the rapid transformation she is bringing to Bangladesh. She is working on projects to improve public transport by introducing metro rail and bus rapid transit.

Bangladesh is now self-sufficient in food production. Around 31.50 lakh elderly people have already come under the safety net programme under her leadership.

Sheikh Hasina started several vocational centres for teaching different skills to both men and women to make employment possible. She is appreciated worldwide for her efforts to improve the condition of women. Now Bangladesh has a booming garment industry as well.

The government under Sheikh Hasina has planted a number of trees in the coastal regions. The business magazine, *Fortune*, ranked Sheikh Hasina 10th among fifty leaders in the world who are transforming the world and inspiring others to do the same.

DID YOU KNOW?

- As many as nineteen attempts have been made to assassinate Sheikh Hasina.
- Her grandmother was so protective about her that she would not even allow her to go to school.

SHEIKH MOHAMMED BIN RASHID

Sheikh Mohammed bin Rashid, the ruler of Dubai, transformed the island nation into the progressive global city that it is today. His meticulous planning and engaged governance has set a new benchmark in the entire Arabian world and is seen as a reference point for development.

EARLY LIFE

Mohammed bin Rashid al Maktum was born on 15 July 1949. He is the third son of Sheikh Rashid bin Saeed Al Maktoum who hailed from the ruling Al Maktoum family. His mother, Latifa bint Hamdan Al Nahyan, was from the royal family.

Right from an early age, Sheikh Mohammed was tutored at home in Arabic and Islamic Studies. His formal education began at Al Ahmedia School and then at the age of ten, he moved to Al Shaab School. After two years, he joined the Dubai Secondary School, and in 1966, he became a student of the Bell Educational Trust's English Language School in Britain. Thereafter, he joined the Mons Officer Cadet School in Aldershot and passed out with the Sword of Honour as the top Commonwealth student. He followed this by training as a pilot in Italy.

In January 1968, Sheikh Mohammed bin Rashid, ruler of Dubai, and Sheikh Zayed, ruler of Abu Dhabi, met in the desert between Dubai and Abu Dhabi to agree to the formation of a United Arab Emirates (UAE). Sheikh Mohammed bin Rashid was appointed as its first minister of defence.

After returning from military training, Sheikh Mohammed's father appointed him as the head of both the Dubai Defence Force and the Dubai Police Force. They were later combined as the Union Defence Force.

VARIOUS BUSINESS VENTURES

Sheikh Mohammed was the man behind the transition of Dubai. He launched the Emirates Airline and also expanded the Dubai Airport which houses some of the largest Boeings and Airbuses in the world. He improved the economic condition of the country through his two companies—Dubai World and Dubai Holding, which manage various projects like hospitality, business parks and real estates. These various companies have employed a number of people across the globe. He also formed the Dubai Ports Authority by merging various ports.

RULER OF DUBAI

Sheikh Mohammed became the ruler of Dubai on 4 January 2006. He then became the vice president of the UAE. He has initiated many reforms since then. He established a process of coordination and strategic planning in the government.

Education and research have been given a lot of emphasis by him. The Mohammed bin Rashid School of Government was established to help create effective public policy. His policies on gender equality and promoting the rights of women make him a 'Messiah' of women in the Middle East.

PHILANTHROPIST RULER

Sheikh Mohammed is seen as a great humanitarian and his initiatives have greatly helped improve the quality of life of people. He has implemented around 1,400 development programmes that have helped millions of people across the globe. Sheikh Mohammed has addressed a wide range of issues, ranging from basic needs to education and from community needs to nurturing the dreams of people. He sought to extend his humanitarian work at the global level since he realized that UAE cannot live or progress as an island. He transformed Dubai into a global city and his progressive mind continues to help the country scale new heights.

DID YOU KNOW?

- Sheikh Mohammed is an established Arabic poet and has been writing since his school days.
- One of his greatest passions is to drive his car despite being in a position to go around in chauffeur-driven cars.
- He owns the largest horse-breeding operation in the world.

SHEIKH MUJIBUR RAHMAN

Sheikh Mujibur Rahman strived relentlessly to give identity to the people of his country, Bangladesh. He was fondly called 'Bangabandhu', which means 'friend of Bengal'.

EARLY LIFE
Sheikh Mujibur Rahman was born on 17 March 1920 in Tungipara, India (now Bangladesh). He was one of six children of Sheikh Lutfur Rahman and Saira Begum. Mujibhur was enrolled into a school in 1927, but had to be withdrawn owing to his eye surgery.

THE ACTIVIST
Mujibur enrolled at the Islamia College and actively participated in students' politics. The cause of a separate Muslim state was one of the main agendas then.

During the partition of India, Mujibur was in Calcutta and endeavoured hard to subdue the communal violence and safeguard the Muslims. After partition, he returned to East Pakistan.

An order was passed by the government on 26 January 1949 that only the language Urdu would be the official state language of Pakistan; however, Bengalis were a majority in East Pakistan. This order was met with vehement opposition, and Mujibur organized various protests for this for which he was imprisoned.

THE POLITICIAN
Mujibur Rehman founded the East Pakistan Awami Muslim League. He was apprehensive about maintaining the identity of the Bengalis and also about preserving their language. When martial law was imposed, Mujibur expressed dissent, but was soon imprisoned. After his release, he formed the party Swadhin Bangla Biplobi Porishad to check the injustice meted out by Ayub Khan who was the president

of Pakistan from 1958 to 1969. He started dreaming of Bangladesh as a free nation.

THE STRATEGIST

There were mass protests against Pakistan's denial of democracy. In 1966, Mujibur came up with a six-point plan in which his main demands were self-government and autonomy for East Pakistan in political, economic and defence fronts. He was able to generate the support of his people. He announced that East Pakistan would henceforth be called Bangladesh. Thus, he got the title of 'Bangabandhu'.

INCEPTION OF BANGLADESH

A civil disobedience movement was pioneered by Mujibur in 1971 to retaliate against the denial to form the government at the centre despite the Awami League winning a majority in 1970. Mujibur's demand was for the independence of Bangladesh, and the country's freedom was finally declared on 26 March 1971. He was first elected as the prime minister and later as the president of the provincial Bangladesh.

CONSTRUCTION OF A NEW NATION

A new country was born and the responsibility to nurture it properly came upon Mujibur. A new constitution was created based on the tenets of 'nationalism, secularism, democracy and socialism'. He laid emphasis on improving the economic conditions, education, sanitation and the basic necessities of the country.

Rehabilitation of the displaced people was a huge challenge and image construction of this new country was the need of the hour.

Mujibur helped the country to be a part of the UN. He travelled to various countries in Europe, visited the US and Britain to obtain funds and assistance. Mujibur opined that he would always be indebted to India for the liberation of his country.

TRAGEDY AND DEATH

Mujibur Rehman was charged with favouritism in his governance. He was mostly concerned with national issues and therefore could not devote time to local issues which spiralled and were the cause of unrest among the multitude.

On 15 August 1975, tragedy struck Mujibur's household when a group of army officers entered with tanks and assassinated him and his entire family. His assassination was plotted by his annoyed Awami League colleagues and military officers.

DID YOU KNOW?

- Mujibur's historic 7 March speech is recognized as the 'world's all-time best'.
- Mujibur's stature was so high that Fidel Castro compared him to the Himalayas.
- There is an international football tournament organized by the Bangladesh Football Federation (BFF) called Banglabandhu Cup.

SHINZŌ ABE

Shinzo Abe, the prime minister of Japan, is the man behind the phenomenal rise of the country. He is the man who conceived a new form of economics in Japan—Abenomics.

EARLY LIFE

Shinzo Abe was born on 21 September 1954 in Nagato, Japan, into a political family. His grandfather and uncle were prime ministers too. His father was the country's minister of foreign affairs. Abe became interested in politics at an early age.

ENTERING POLITICS

He joined the Liberal Democratic Party in 1982 and became an assistant executive to the minister of foreign affairs. His father passed away in 1991 and Abe realized that he had to establish himself in the political arena and live up to the legacy of the family.

Abe got elected to the House of Representatives in 1993. Since the beginning, he exhibited enterprising leadership qualities. He rose in position within the party and was soon appointed the secretary general of the Liberal Democratic Party. In 2002, Abe was chosen to lead the negotiation on behalf of the families of thirteen Japanese citizens abducted by North Korea in the 1970s and 1980s.

PREMIER OF JAPAN

Abe was elected as the prime minister in 2006. He was always a leader who thought of the people first; therefore, on assuming his duties, he sought ways to balance the budget by curtailing expenditure and not increasing taxes.

In order to invoke the feeling of nationalism among young minds, he initiated certain changes in the textbooks of Japan, wherein the content should speak about Japanese culture, patriotism and pride in ancient history.

While Abe maintained good relations with India, China, Taiwan, the US, etc. he maintained stern ties with North Korea and was always sceptical of the latter's intentions. He has strived tremendously to strengthen the defence of his country. He even upgraded the defence portfolio and gave it full ministry status with all the powers and facilities. Abe resigned from office on 26 September 2007 due to ill health.

ABENOMICS AND SECOND INNINGS

Shinzo Abe was elected as the prime minister for the second time on 26 December 2012. He swore to bring a revolution in the country's economy. He said that he had to put the progress of the nation on a fast track and declared, 'Japan is back.'

Shinzo Abe's economic strategies, called 'Abenomics', are broadly based on a strategic monetary policy, increased government spending and private investments. It has been the aim of Shinzo Abe since the beginning to liberate Japan from its stagnant economy. He has always wanted to do away with deflation and increase the demand of Japanese goods worldwide. By 2017, the unemployment rate dropped to below 3 percent for the first time in twenty-three years under his reign. The growth rate of the country has changed from a negative to a positive one.

Shinzo Abe has proven to be a very effective leader. He has opened up more universities and institutes, and has initiated positive changes in education. He was elected as the prime minister for the third time on 24 December 2014 and for the fourth term in 2017. He is continuing with his various plans of growth. Under his leadership, Japan has managed to break free from the economic stagnation of the past and is soaring high as a high-potential country in the world.

DID YOU KNOW?

- Abe has great interest in archery and likes to try his hand at it sometimes.
- He is the first prime minister of Japan to visit the Arizona Warship which was destroyed by the Japanese in the Pearl Harbour incident.
- Shinzo Abe is fond of Manga comics, a famous comic series of Japan.

SIMÓN BOLÍVAR

Simón Bolívar was a crusader who was honoured by Americans of both the continents as he had liberated five South American republics.

EARLY LIFE

Simón Bolívar was born on 24 July 1783 in Caracas, present day Venezuela, into a luxurious home of a wealthy colonial family. Growing up during the greater part of his childhood at his father's estate made him aware about class differences.

Seeing the victims of Spanish rule and how they were oppressed to abject poverty, he decided to dedicate his life to the cause of the downtrodden. One of his tutors, Simón Rodriguez, had a deep influence on him. Rodriguez introduced him to the world of renaissance and liberal thought. After the death of his parents in 1799, Bolívar went to Spain and continued his education.

REVOLUTIONARY

The world was rapidly changing in the early 18th century with countries rising up into revolution and demanding liberty. This was the time that Bolívar travelled to many parts of the world and gathered insight into life. Perhaps it was during his visit to the US that the dream of a union of two American continents came to him.

Beginning 1810, complete freedom was demanded by one colony after another in South America. Bolívar led a group of people in Venezuela and declared independence. Their declaration of independence was officially ratified on 5 July 1811. In 1814, Bolívar was forced into exile when Ferdinand VII, the king of Spain, was determined to crush the revolution in South America.

FIGHT FOR FREEDOM

After learning King Ferdinand's plan, Bolívar returned to Venezuela with some men to start a ten-year long struggle with the king. His mission was not simply to liberate Venezuela but to free five of its colonies. They were New Granada (Colombia), Ecuador, Peru, Upper Peru (Bolivia) and, of course, Venezuela. To liberate New Granada in 1819, Bolívar's army crossed the swampy valley of Orinoco. They also did the daring act of scaling the 400m barrier of the Andes Mountains. Finally, in Bogota, Bolívar and his men beat the Spanish Army which was twice the size of their army. New Granada was free, and Bolívar was hailed as the liberator.

New Granada merged with Venezuela to form Grand Colombia, and Bolívar was its president. But his task was not complete yet. In 1821, near Caracas, the liberator drove away the Spanish Forces from Venezuela forever. With the assistance of the able officer, Antonio Jose de Sucre, Bolívar won the liberty of Ecuador on 24 May 1822.

FINAL LIBERATION

Next, Bolívar turned all his attention to Peru. It was then that he met the great Argentinean revolutionary, José de San Martin. Bolívar claimed that meeting this legendary man was a great accomplishment of his life. San Martin was the liberator of Argentina and Chile. San Martin left the task of liberating Peru to Bolívar. When the Spanish Army surrendered in Peru and Upper Peru, the liberation and independence of South America was complete. All the five nations were united under the Union of Gran Colombia.

Simon Bolívar will always be remembered as the great liberator. There are very few figures in world history who can match his rare qualities. Bolívar breathed his last on 17 December 1830. He has been honoured as the father of five nations.

DID YOU KNOW?

- Bolívar devoted all his fortune to the revolutionary cause of South America.
- The country Bolivia is named after him.
- He is known by the title 'El Libertador', which means 'Great Liberator'.

SIRIMAVO BANDARANAIKE

irimavo Bandaranaike was the world's first female prime minister. She took over the position when women were not considered fit to rule. She has been called the 'Iron Lady' of Sri Lanka.

EARLY LIFE

Sirimavo Bandaranaike was born as Sirima Ratwatte in Kandy, Sri Lanka on 17 April 1916. Sirimavo's father, Barnes Ratwatte Dissawa, was a member of the State Council in the senate of Ceylon (now Sri Lanka). Rosalind Mahawelatenne Kumarihamy, her mother, belonged to the royal family. After schooling, Sirimavo became engaged in social work. She grew up in a political environment.

ENTERING POLITICS

Sirimavo Bandaranaike's entry into politics was sudden and eventful. In 1959, her husband Solomon, the then prime minister of Sri Lanka, was assassinated by a Buddhist monk. Besides, Sri Lanka Freedom Party was on the verge of collapsing. Sirimavo rose to the occasion and swiftly established herself as the undisputed leader of the Sri Lanka Freedom Party. In 1960, Sirimavo Bandaranaike became the prime minister of Sri Lanka, making history as the first female leader to head a national government in the whole world. Although Sirimavo's political opponents often criticized her for capitalizing on her husband's assassination to rise to power by emotionally exploiting people, Sirimavo grew from strength to strength to become the prime minister of Sri Lanka again in 1970.

CONTRIBUTION

During her tenure, Sirimavo transformed Sri Lanka into an economy that nationalized important sectors like banking and insurance. She brought schools run by the Roman Catholic Church under government control. Sirimavo also pursued efforts to make Sinhalese the sole national language of the country. However, this move is believed to have deeply alienated the nation's Tamil speakers. Her penchant for Sinhalese was so intense that she went ahead and changed the university admissions policy to benefit the Sinhalese, putting Tamilians at a great disadvantage. She advocated Buddhism and furthered Sinhalese culture.

FOREIGN RELATIONS

Sirimavo's international relations were unique and she aligned neither with the east nor with the west. She wanted to maintain the unique character of Sri Lanka. The government's takeover of foreign businesses offended many foreign investors, especially Britain and the US. Therefore, she established trade relations with China and USSR. She mediated a major role in mitigating the India-China border issue in 1962.

Sri Lanka's relationship with India was strained for some time when Sirimavo ordered the deportation of many Tamilians staying in Sri Lanka. She signed the 'Sirimavo-Shastri Pact' in October 1964 at New Delhi, thereby agreeing to provide citizenship and deport Tamilians staying there on a proportionate basis.

In the later years of her political career, Sirimavo promoted her daughter Chandrika Kumaratunga as her political heir. Chandrika went on to become the president of Sri Lanka even as Sirimavo Bandaranaike occupied the prime minister's position, a ceremonial position under the constitution that was adopted for Sri Lanka in 1978.

Sirimavo remained active in politics after her retirement and died of a heart attack after casting her vote on 10 October 2000, only two months after retiring from office.

DID YOU KNOW?

- Sirimavo was so particular about her national dress that she insisted on wearing the Lama saree even when she volunteered in Girls' Guide, instead of the regular school uniform.
- Her favourite sport was tennis and she used to play whenever she could find time.
- The 'vo' in the name Sirimavo means respect.

SUBHAS CHANDRA BOSE

Arguably India's most revered freedom fighter, Subhas Chandra Bose was a charismatic personality who is celebrated by the young and old even today.

EARLY LIFE
Born on 23 January 1897 in Cuttack to Prabhavati Devi and Janakinath Bose, Subhas did his schooling from the Protestant European School. Subhas was a sensitive child and was disturbed by how the Indians had to suffer discrimination at the hands of the British. Subhas was particularly fond of Swami Vivekananda's philosophy.

In 1913, Bose joined Presidency College at Calcutta. He was expelled from the college as he protested against his history teacher for making anti-India comments. Later, Bose graduated in philosophy from Scottish Church College. He also went on to clear the Imperial Civil Service exam in England but did not take up a job with the British.

ASSOCIATION WITH THE INDIAN NATIONAL CONGRESS
Subhas Chandra Bose met Gandhiji in 1921 and participated in the non-cooperation movement. He started the newspaper, *Swaraj*, and was the editor of the newspaper, *Forward*, founded by Chittaranjan Das. In 1923, Bose was elected the president of the All India Youth Congress. During this time, he served several stints in prison for his nationalist activities.

FALL OUT WITH THE CONGRESS
Subhas Chandra Bose belonged to the new school of thought which believed in complete self-rule, unlike the moderate old school. Due to his difference of opinion with Gandhiji, Bose resigned in 1939 and formed a new party named 'The Forward Bloc'.

FORMATION OF INA

When the Second World War broke out, Subhas Chandra Bose organized mass protests against the British in Calcutta. There was tremendous response to his call, 'Give me blood and I will give you freedom'. He was put under house arrest. In January 1941, Bose escaped and reached Berlin via Peshawar.

Bose felt that the main enemies of British imperialism—Nazi Germany, fascist Italy and Japan—should be utilized to their advantage. He, therefore, went from Germany to Japan to Burma gathering support, and assumed command of over 40,000 soldiers recruited from Singapore and other South East Asian regions, which he called the Indian National Army (INA).

Bose led the army and not only won back the Andaman and Nicobar Islands from the British but also established the Azad Hind government there. An Indian tricolour, modelled after the flag of the Indian National Congress, was raised for the first time in the town of Moirang, in Manipur, in north-eastern India. But, he had to stop his army from advancing further, as his main supporting nations, Germany and Japan, surrendered during the Second World War.

POLITICAL IDEOLOGY

Bose had firm faith in democracy and dreamt of an independent India. He believed that freedom cannot be served on a platter, rather Indians had to usurp it from the British. Subhas Chandra Bose derived immense inspiration from the Bhagavad Gita during his struggle against the British.

DEATH AND LEGACY

Subhas Chandra Bose died reportedly due to receiving third degree burns during a plane crash on 18 August 1945. He seemed to have disappeared mysteriously after retreating from the north-eastern states of India. However, his death continues to remain a mystery.

DID YOU KNOW?

- He is called the Father of the Indian National Army as he is the one who started Azad Hind Fauj, an armed force to fight against the British.
- He is popularly and fondly called 'Netaji' by his followers.
- Subhas went to meet Hitler, who was extremely impressed with his courage.

SWAMI VIVEKANANDA

Swami Vivekananda was a monk who has left an indelible mark on Indians and millions across the world. His legacy is that of deep knowledge, respect for cultures and racial equanimity.

EARLY LIFE
Narendranath Dutta was born on 12 January 1863 to a respected lawyer, Vishwanath Dutta, and Bhubaneshwari Devi, devoted to God. Little did they know that this young boy would take the world on a journey of spiritual consciousness. He was fascinated by the wandering monks and sadhus and would offer them whatever he had.

INTELLECTUAL GROWTH
Narendranath attended the Scottish Church College between 1881 and 1884. He grew into an intellectual and joined the Brahmo Samaj, a Hindu reform organization that protested against orthodox practices in Hinduism. Narendranath's quest for the truth grew, and he began to look for ways of knowing the ultimate truth, knowing God.

MEETING RAMAKRISHNA PARAMAHANSA
Witnessing Narendranath's desire for knowing the truth, his professor referred him to Ramakrishna Paramahansa. The meeting was a strange one as both of them talked as if they had known each other for years. When Narendranath asked him whether he had seen God, Ramakrishana replied to his surprise that he could see God. After completing college, his spiritual learning went on under Ramakrishna for four years wherein Narendranath learnt about the Vedanta, Bhakti Yoga and Gyan Yoga. Tragedy struck in 1885 when Ramakrishna was diagnosed with throat cancer. Just before the passing away of the guru, Narendranath experienced the Nirvakalpa Samadhi, which means the total dissolution of the self to the supreme or Brahman.

HEAD OF RAMAKRISHNA ORDER

Narendranath was established as the head of the Ramakrishna Order in 1886. By 1887, they had established a 'math' or monastery at Baranagar near Calcutta. All the monks renounced material life and were given a new name. Narendranath was henceforth known as Swami Vivekananda.

TRAVELLING ACROSS INDIA

Swami Vivekananda started to tour India in 1888 to understand the real essence of the country. He travelled through Rajasthan, Gujarat and many parts of South India. Frustrated at the suffering he saw—be it debt, poverty, hunger or abuse of religion, he went to Kanyakumari and swam to a big rock where he meditated for three days. He sought to find answers as to why India had reached that state. In his meditation, he realized that India would rise only through the restoration of that highest spiritual consciousness which had made her the cradle of all nations. Upliftment of the downtrodden masses and inculcating a sense of service were the only ways to regain the lost glory.

SPREADING VEDANTA AND FOUNDING THE RAMAKRISHNA MISSION

On 31 May 1893, Swami Vivekananda set sail for the US to spread the message of Hindu dharma and universal oneness. He addressed the Parliament of Religions held in Chicago and began his speech with 'Sisters and brothers of America'. He went with the unique message of how all religions are one and lead to God. Swamiji's words reflected his direct experience of the divine and thus captivated the entire world. Vivekananda returned to India in 1897 and founded the Ramakrishna Mission at Belur Math near Calcutta. Its primary objective was to serve the poor and distressed. It also established schools, colleges, hospitals and propagated the tenets of Vedanta.

Swami Vivekananda attained mahasamadhi on 4 July 1902 after teaching the world the great lessons of humanity and brotherhood.

DID YOU KNOW?

- Narendranath was a very restless child and when he used to be out of control, his mother used to pour cold water on him and chant 'Shiva' to calm him.
- Swamiji travelled across India on foot.
- Young Narendranath had memorized Sanskrit grammar, the Ramayana and the Mahabharata.

THEODORE ROOSEVELT

A man of contrasts, Theodore Roosevelt, the legendary president of the US, had the qualities of a legislator as well as a cowboy. An explorer and a governor, he taught others how to live a complete and meaningful life.

EARLY LIFE

Roosevelt was born on 27 October 1858 in New York City to Theodore Roosevelt Sr and Martha. His family owned a successful plate-glass import business. Roosevelt was a sickly, delicate boy who suffered from asthma, and yet he loved to be outdoors and was fascinated by any wild creature that came his way.

Roosevelt did his schooling from his home, as his health did not allow him to go outdoors much.

Roosevelt realized quite young that the frailty of his body could be overcome only by courage and will power. He was able to transform himself from a weak child to a strong man. He enrolled himself into Harvard in 1876.

ENTRY INTO POLITICS

Politics was considered improper for a gentleman during those times but Roosevelt found his calling in it. He said, 'If they are running the country, I want to have a part in it.' He worked hard for republican candidates and was soon awarded with his first nomination for office. In November 1881, he was elected the youngest member of the state assembly and entered the corrupt world of New York politics. He challenged the prevalent corruption and sought to change the system.

PRESIDENTSHIP

President William McKinley was assassinated in 1901, and forty-two-year-old Roosevelt, who was then the vice president, was appointed the president. Ready to bring reforms, in his first term, he proposed the 'Square Deal', which was a domestic programme aimed at bringing reforms at the American workplace, government regulation of industry and consumer protection. He realized that the US could not exist as an island.

Roosevelt improved public relations. He revamped the US Navy and created the 'Great White Fleet', sending it on a world tour proclaiming the glory and power of the US.

SECOND TERM

To be re-elected for the second term, Roosevelt knew that he had to go directly to the people. He toured the country and delivered a number of speeches. A large and enthusiastic crowd gathered to cheer Roosevelt on his landslide victory as the president of the US. He got the Panama Canal built, a technical genius that connected the Atlantic Ocean with the Pacific.

POST PRESIDENTSHIP

Roosevelt was requested to run for a third term, but he refused. He wanted to retire and relax. He sailed for Africa on an extended safari. He toured the continent for eleven months and indulged in nature study. After that, he visited Europe where he was given a warm welcome everywhere.

Roosevelt returned to New York in 1910 and spent most of his time studying nature and indulging in field trips.

In the early morning of 6 January 1919, Roosevelt died in his sleep.

DID YOU KNOW?

- A boxing injury in the White House had left him blind in one eye.
- He was the first president to refer to the presidential mansion as the White House.
- Roosevelt was the first president to host a black man for dinner and appoint a Jewish person as a cabinet minister.

THOMAS JEFFERSON

He was one of the most important people of the American independence and the author of the Declaration of Independence. The third president of the US, Thomas Jefferson, is an iconic figure of the world.

EARLY LIFE

Thomas Jefferson was born on 13 April 1743 in Virginia. Jefferson's father was the first person to lay down the map of the province of Virginia.

As a young boy, Jefferson's favourite pastimes were playing in the woods, reading books and playing the violin. He studied law under the tutelage of George Wythe, who was a respected Virginia attorney.

DECLARATION OF INDEPENDENCE

Thomas Jefferson was one of the most fervent supporters of American independence. His political work, *A Summary View of the Rights of British America,* established him as an eloquent advocate of American freedom.

The year 1774 saw the drafting of a very important document which justified the rights of Americans to govern themselves. Jefferson was chosen as a delegate to the Second Continental Congress and was given the task of writing the first draft of the Declaration of Independence which he finished in June 1776. This declaration explained, in a detailed manner, why thirteen colonies wanted to be free from British rule.

The US became the first country to declare its independence from the colonial rule in the modern era. This draft became a role model for further declarations of independence all over the world.

ENTERING POLITICS

During the years of revolution, Jefferson returned to Virginia and the twenty-five-year-old was elected to the Virginia House of Delegates. While serving as the governor of Virginia, he came up with another important draft. He authored the Virginia Statute for Religious Freedom, one of his most significant achievements. It later served as the forerunner to the First Amendment to the US constitution, protecting the right of an individual to worship as they choose.

In 1785, Jefferson succeeded Benjamin Franklin as the US minister to France. This required him to travel and stay in Europe frequently. When he returned after five years, he wrote to his friend, 'My God! How little do my countrymen know what precious blessings they are in possession of, and which no other people on earth enjoy.' Jefferson wanted to assert that America was in no way lesser than Europe.

PRESIDENCY

In 1800, Thomas Jefferson was elected as the third president of the US. One of the many significant achievements of Jefferson was the purchase of Louisiana territory from France which doubled the size of the US. He then sent out experts to gather information about the place, during which important information about the natives, flora and fauna was found.

Jefferson started his second term in 1804. He set up the US Military Academy which was a formal institution for scientific and military learning. In his annual message in 1806, he called for the criminalization of international slave trade. This act prohibited import of slaves and was a landmark decision.

Education was considered to be of utmost importance for nation-building. He wanted education to be separate from the church, wherein the students could choose their desired subjects. Jefferson not only founded the University of Virginia but also designed it.

POST-PRESIDENCY AND LEGACY

Jefferson refused to run for a third term. He spent his post-presidential years at his house, Monticello, where he continued to pursue his interests. These included music, gardening, architecture and reading. Jefferson died on 4 July 1826 which was coincidentally the 50th anniversary of the Declaration of Independence.

DID YOU KNOW?

- Jefferson was a voracious reader, and his personal library contained around 6,487 books.
- Jefferson's house, Monticello, had thirty-three rooms over four floors and took forty years to build.
- He had mockingbirds as pets, and his favourite was named Dick.

TSHERING TOBGAY

Tshering Tobgay, the first prime minister of Bhutan, ushered in a new era to the Shangri-la of the world. It was an era of growth, development and making a mark in the world.

EARLY LIFE
Tshering Tobgay was born on 19 September 1965 in the district of Haa, Bhutan. His father was in the Bhutanese Army and Tobgay is the eldest of six sons. Tobgay got a scholarship from the UN for studying abroad. After graduation, he went on to seek a master's degree in public administration in 2004.

EARLY CAREER
Tobgay returned home with many ideas of development and growth. He established the National Technical Authority and served as its director. He contributed largely towards improving the quality of vocational and technical education in Bhutan. Having served the nation at various posts, he thought to resign from the Ministry of Labour in 2007 and take up greater challenges.

SIGNING THE CONSTITUTION
Tobgay played a major role in signing the constitution of the country. After the king declared democracy and the end of monarchy in Bhutan, a new constitution was made. Tobgay considers himself extremely lucky for being chosen by the king as the one to sign the new document. The constitution emphasized the importance of saving the environment and finding various other ways to safeguard the unique culture of this tiny Himalayan country.

ENTERING POLITICS
Tobgay entered politics with the intention of helping the king, as

he had established democracy in Bhutan. He founded the People's Democratic Party which was the first registered party in Bhutan. He ran for the parliamentary election in 2008 and was the leader of the Opposition in the Bhutan parliament from 2008 to 2013.

In the elections held in 2013, Tobgay was elected as the prime minister of Bhutan. His main agenda in the campaign was to help the common man by addressing issues such as electricity, and national ambulance scooters. He said that people needed facilities more than the Gross National Happiness. He did not undermine the happiness of the people but wanted to transform their life for a better tomorrow.

CONTRIBUTION

Tshering Tobgay believed in establishing contact with the rest of the world. He is well known for his speeches at the world stage which are full of substance and add a new understanding of Bhutan.

Tobgay is an environmentalist, not simply because the constitution demands the leader to be so, but because he genuinely feels so. He has proudly claimed to the world, on several occasions, about Bhutan being carbon negative.

Bhutan's main economy is agriculture and generating hydro-electric power. Tobgay has signed the 'B to B' (Bhutan to Bharat and Bharat to Bhutan) pact with India wherein Bhutan would supply electricity to India. India would extend help in providing an e-library, educational scholarships, etc.

The economy of the country is still weak and has to import many things. Bhutan has a free market system but it will be a while when it starts exporting its goods to other countries.

Tobgay often interacts with the common Bhutanese to understand their needs properly. Under his leadership, Bhutan will surely scale new heights and will be an inspiration to the world.

BALANCING MONARCHY AND DEMOCRACY

Bhutan is a unique nation where despite democracy, people still look up to the king. Even the prime minister draws inspiration from him. The monarchy in Bhutan is the conscience of Bhutan, always guiding the nation correctly.

DID YOU KNOW?

- Tobgay's hobbies are reading, trekking, archery and music.
- He is quite tech-savvy, and an avid blogger. He has also participated in a TED Talk on 'Key to Happiness'.
- Tobgay is the recipient of the lifetime scarf, the 'Lungmar Scarf', by His Majesty for his contribution in establishing the democratic procedures of the country.

VLADIMIR LENIN

L enin is considered to be one of the most influential and powerful leaders of the 20th century. Fascinated by his brain, there have been many studies to find out what made him such a genius.

EARLY LIFE
Vladimir Ilich Ulyanov was born on 10 April 1870 in Simbersk, in central Russia. His father was an inspector of schools. Young Lenin was a lively child, a debater and loved to learn foreign languages.

Lenin grew up at a time when discontent was growing among people owing to the miserable living conditions. Life took a different turn for him when his elder brother, Aleksandr, a university student at that time, was executed for being a part of a conspiracy to kill the Czar. As the brother of a terrorist, Lenin was closely watched.

BECOMING A REVOLUTIONARY
Karl Marx had a great impact on Lenin and he declared himself a Marxist in 1889. Lenin soon moved to St Petersburg and formed a group with other Marxists. Aiming to agitate the factory workers, they distributed leaflets and also listened to the workers' grievances. Consequentially, Lenin was arrested.

Lenin continued to write revolutionary pamphlets even from prison. This earned him a further exile of three years in Siberia.

THE REVOLUTION
Lenin moved to Munich to carry on with his plan of a revolution. His writings were smuggled to Russia by his followers. A peaceful march in 1905 proved to be a turning point. There were demonstrations held by factory workers demanding better working, conditions. The Czar's police opened fire without any warning, which led to many deaths, and the day became known as 'Bloody Sunday'. Lenin saw

an opportunity in the consequent nationwide protests to turn them into action against the government. He distributed pamphlets about how to turn the protests violent, which then forced the Czar to announce some reforms. The revolution was over and Lenin had to flee Russia to avoid the Czar's police. But Lenin never gave up.

WORLD WAR I

Lenin saw the war as a great revolutionary opportunity and wrote encouraging write-ups for soldiers of all nations. The war was a disaster for Russia as they lost almost every battle. In 1917, the angry people spilled out onto the streets and turned violent against the government. Within a week, the Czar had to forego his position and Russia celebrated.

COMMUNIST GOVERNMENT

In October 1917, Lenin and his comrades declared a revolution against the provincial government formed by Aleksandr Kerensky. Lenin announced that Russia was a communist nation and he was their leader. Lenin ended the war with Germany and Russia had to pay a heavy price in terms of land.

Lenin tried to bring in a new policy to improve the economic condition of the country. He initiated some private enterprises but they were not enough to recover the huge losses that were incurred due to war. Moreover, as per government policies, the businessmen could only own small industries, and not factories. There was scarcity of food in the country and Lenin found it difficult to meet the needs of the people. Lenin's activities were hindered by his deteriorating health as he was having frequent strokes which left him almost paralyzed. Lenin's fourth stroke killed him in January 1924. The city of St Petersberg was renamed as Leningrad in his memory.

DID YOU KNOW?

- Lenin's body has been preserved, and hundreds of people flock to pay homage to him.
- Lenin loved to listen to Beethoven, but he stopped listening to him as he feared that it would make him soft.
- Lenin learnt to play chess from his father. He was so good that he used to play with multiple players at the same time.

VLADIMIR PUTIN

Putin's colossal rise from an unemployed spy to the modern day Czar has surprised many. He is the Russian leader who has managed to expand his hold and make his presence felt effectively in the western hemisphere.

EARLY LIFE
Vladimir Vladimirovich Putin was born on 7 October 1952 in Leningrad, Russia. His mother was a kind lady and his father worked as a security guard. He graduated from Leningrad State University with a law degree in 1975.

CAREER IN KGB
After Putin's graduation, he joined the Komitet Gosudarstvennoy Bezopasnosti (KGB) or the Committee for State Security as an intelligence officer. The main function of KGB was to closely monitor the operations and functions of Russian citizens. He returned to Russia from Dresde, East Germany in 1989 and by then the KGB was almost falling apart.

ENTRY INTO POLITICS
After the fall of communism in 1991, he became an advisor to politician Anatoly Sobchak who had been his professor. He was appointed the director of the Federal Security Service (FSB), the KGB's domestic successor, under President Boris Yeltsin in 1998. He rose through ranks while working under him. The real boost was when Yeltsin made Putin the prime minister in 1999.

PRESIDENT OF RUSSIA
Boris Yeltsin stepped down from the post of president and Putin was elected the president in March 2000.

In his first presidential speech, he said that he wanted Russia to be a free, prosperous and civilized country; a country that its citizens are proud of and is respected internationally. Putin used his power to advocate certain international policies especially with regard to arms treaty and relations with China. He focused mainly on economic reforms and sought to revive the dipping economy of the country.

SECOND TERM

In 2004, the Russians re-elected Putin for his second term as the president. The relentless efforts of Putin were showing results and Russia was gradually moving towards economic boom.

Putin made a trip to Israel which was the first ever trip by a Russian leader. The leaders of both the countries discussed about security issues and this meeting led to the strengthening of ties. This positioned Russia as an important country for any discussion of Middle East nations. Putin could not run for the presidential elections for the third time as the constitution forbade it.

PRIME MINISTER OF RUSSIA

Putin was appointed as the prime minister of Russia in 2008 by an executive order. Apart from resolving the global economic crisis, he was concerned with the dipping population of Russia. However, things started to be better in 2010 and Russia's population began to grow, owing to the economic reforms of Putin. He also made the smart move of joining the World Trade Organization, a step taken after a discussion of two decades.

He has also taken a number of measures for developing the agricultural sector. Grain growers, livestock farmers and processing companies have come up.

THIRD TERM AS THE PRESIDENT

President Dmitry Medvedev proposed the name of Putin for the post of president saying that it was necessary for the larger interest of the nation. Putin was elected the President for the third time in 2012. He has taken many important decisions after coming to power. Salaries of public sector employees have increased. Healthcare facilities have improved and so have education and housing. There is also a committee chaired by him to see that whatever has been decided for the betterment of the people is also being executed. He is a powerful leader not only of Russia but of the entire world.

DID YOU KNOW?

- *Time* magazine named Putin as the 'Person of the Year' in 2007 and also the most powerful man from 2013 to 2016.
- Putin loves adventure. He once went 200 feet underwater to pay a 140-year-old shipwreck a visit.
- Once while fishing in Siberia, Putin caught a 46-pound pike, a fish.

WANGARI MAATHAI

Wangari Maathai has been given the adage, 'Eco-Warrior with a smile'. She is a force to reckon with across the world as an activist of human rights and a saviour of the environment.

EARLY LIFE

Wangari Muta Maathai was born on 1 April 1940 in Nyeri, Kenya in a farming family, and learnt the important lesson of respecting the soil and its bounty. Maathai was very close to her mother and grew observant of nature around her like her mother. Being a very bright student, her brother persuaded his parents to send her to school. She did so well that she earned a scholarship to attend college in the US. During her years in the US, she was amazed to see people expressing their perspectives openly. She learnt that people could and should speak out what they believed in. After receiving her master's degree, she returned to Kenya. She completed her doctoral studies in veterinary anatomy and joined as a faculty at the University of Nairobi.

BUDDING ENVIRONMENTALIST

Maathai was drawn to the issues of women and also the depleting environment. The insistence of growing cash crops for more revenue had a damaging effect on the soil. The rural families had no access to firewood; livestock suffered because there was no vegetation to graze on; and streams were drying up creating havoc in the environment. Maathai decided to plant seven trees in 1977. The budding environmentalist quit teaching and formed the Green Belt Movement with a handful of villagers who planted seeds. Soon, this group was joined by many women who eventually created jobs for many others. Women began taking control over their future.

POLITICAL FORCE

With the expansion of Green Belt Movement, she came at a crossroads with the government. She became the spokesperson of environmental reforms. She also started with the mission of educating people that they must demand accountability for managing natural resources from the government. In her first public confrontation with the government, she protested the building of a sixty-storey skyscraper in Nairobi's Uhuru Park and was soon reckoned as a great political force.

ACTIVISM

Maathai soon found herself not only planting trees but also fighting for the restoration of democracy in her country. She vehemently opposed the iron rule of President Daniel arap Moi. 1990s was a time of trials and tribulations for her. She was imprisoned and intimidated several times but continued her protests undaunted.

The political climate of Kenya changed for the better after the 2002 elections. The new government was more considerate towards the issues of women and thus women, in turn, were given more roles to play in policymaking. The Green Belt Movement established the Women for Change (WFC) which aimed at empowering women, especially through education. The WFC also started initiating discussions on passing laws for ensuring the rights of women.

CHAMPION OF PEACE

In 2003, Maathai was appointed as the assistant minister of environment. She took actively to safeguarding women's rights and also the environment. Addressing the UN on several occasions, she spoke on behalf of women and human rights. Her influence was so wide that by 2005, over fifteen African countries had become associated with the Green Belt Movement.

In 2004, Maathai was awarded with the Nobel Peace Prize to applaud her services to the protection of the environment and human rights. She was the first environmentalist to win this prize. Although she breathed her last on 25 September 2011, the world has many more Maathais following her footsteps.

DID YOU KNOW?

- Maathai has planted more than 30 million trees across Africa.
- Maathai was the first woman to earn a doctorate degree in Central Africa and the first female to become a professor in a university.
- Maathai enrolled into primary school at the age of eight.

WINSTON CHURCHILL

Winston Churchill was a statesman, journalist, historian and an extremely intelligent politician with the gift of the gab.

EARLY LIFE

Winston Leonard Spencer Churchill was born on 30 November 1874 in Oxfordshire, England. He spent his childhood in Ireland. He was not a great student until he started attending a military school.

After his graduation, he joined the British Army where he served in the north-western frontier of India and Sudan. However, he left the army in 1899 and became a war correspondent.

CHURCHILL AND POLITICS

Churchill got the inspiration to join politics from his father. He switched from Conservative Party to Liberal party and was elected as a member of parliament in 1908. He introduced various reforms including fixing a minimum wage for labourers and unemployment insurance.

Churchill was appreciated for being instrumental in passing the bill for People's Budget which meant that the wealthy would pay taxes for new social welfare programmes. Churchill also took initiative in modernizing the British Navy and also setting up the Royal Navy Air Service. In 1911, he was named as the First Lord of the Admiralty, a great honour bestowed upon him by the British Navy.

CHURCHILL AS THE PRIME MINISTER

Churchill made great contributions as the prime minister of Britain. He remained in office from 1940 to 1945. When Hitler rose to power and the Second World War was looming over the world, many did not take the threats of the Nazis seriously, but Churchill knew that Britain had to be sufficiently armed to face any challenge. He mobilized the other European nations through his speeches and radio interviews to have hope. He made the others realize that the threat of Hitler was not only to the island nation but to the world.

On 18 June 1940, Churchill declared in his speech that 'the battle of Britain' was about to begin. Churchill was a remarkable statesman. Thus, he formed an association with the US and the Soviet Union. When Nazi Germany attacked the USSR, Churchill extended his support. He worked closely with the US President Roosevelt and Soviet Union leader Joseph Stalin with whom he created strategies to oust the Axis powers. It was because of this concerted effort that Germany was compelled to surrender in 1945; although the same year, Churchill lost the general elections.

SECOND INNINGS

Churchill became the prime minister for the second time in 1951. Post world wars, a lot of reforms and improvement was required in various sectors. To establish standard housing system, Churchill made some amendments. He also passed the Mines and Quarries Act to improve the working conditions of the mine workers.

Churchill was fearless and made no compromises when it was for the betterment of his people. He was knighted by Queen Elizabeth II in 1953. The same year, Churchill received the Nobel Prize for Literature for the memoirs he was writing amidst all the ups and downs in his life. Winston Churchill led an eventful life and passed away on 24 January 1965.

DID YOU KNOW?

- Churchill's mother was an American.
- He was a great artist who created more than 500 paintings.
- He loved laying bricks and had built many walls in his house.

XI JINPING

Xi Jinping, the president of the People's Republic of China, is one of the most powerful men in the world and a leader to be reckoned with. It was Jinping's vision that took China to a position of strategic dominance, a feat that none of his predecessors could achieve.

EARLY LIFE

Xi Jinping was born to Xi Zhongxun, a Long March hero who later became a vice-premier, and Qi Xin in June 1953. He grew up amidst the talks of Red Army. He idolized his father and wanted to be someone like him. Things changed when General Mao declared himself as the dictator and his father was humiliated for opposing Mao and the family was put behind bars. Xi fled and took refuge in a cave far away from Beijing. He had a very difficult life there and worked as an agricultural labour and used to sleep on rocks.

ENTERING POLITICS

Xi maintained a very low-key life but had a keen desire to rise to the top. He always kept himself abreast with the political landscape. Repulsed by the corruption in China, he was determined to get rid of it. Xi had tried to join the Communist Party several times but failed because his father had gone against the Party. However, in 1974, he was finally taken into the Party and thus began his political career. He worked at various posts and had many ideas of development. But, his ideas were not accepted.

The death of Mao in 1976 brought in numerous changes in China. The country opened up to capitalism and with it many new possibilities. When he was the Party leader from 1998 to 2000, he invited foreign investments and also revitalized some historical places. Soon his reputation as an honest and enterprising politician spread and he began to be taken seriously. Development followed wherever he went and in 2007 he was chosen to lead the Party in Shanghai.

His time came in 2012 when he became the general secretary of the central committee of the Communist Party of China.

XI AS A PARAMOUNT LEADER

In 2012, Xi was elected as the president and, with his political supremacy, he became the 'Paramount Leader'. Everyone thought that Xi would be an amiable leader but, with time, he has proven that he can take tough decisions when it comes to the development of his country. Once in power, he set to assume these objectives, he set down to tackle issues he had often talked about, including a strong military, better education, better employment opportunities, social security and high medical standards.

He launched a massive crackdown on corruption, previously unheard of in communist history. There were thousands of officials behind bars.

Xi is a pragmatic leader and has sent a positive message to the common Chinese that his government would never crush the dreams of the ordinary people. On being questioned about being authoritative, Xi says that he believes in discipline and without it the Chinese dream can never be realized.

Xi Jinping's political thoughts are now a part of China's party and state constitutions. Jinping has also amended the rules and abolished term limits for the presidency which makes him a president for life. In 2018, *Forbes* ranked Xi as the world's most powerful and influential person.

DID YOU KNOW?

- Xi is an ardent follower of Confucius and has embraced many of his teachings since he came to power.
- He watched the Bollywood movie *Dangal* dubbed in Chinese and loved it.
- He is a fan of *The Godfather* series.

YASSER ARAFAT

Arafat is a symbol of the Palestinian struggle for independence. He dedicated his entire life for the people who had lost their motherland.

EARLY LIFE

Muhammad Abd al-Rauf al-Qudwah al-Husayni, popularly known as Yasser Arafat, was born in Cairo on 24 August 1929. Not much is known about his childhood.

He graduated in civil engineering from Cairo University in 1956. He was drawn to the cause of the Palestinians since his childhood. He dreamt of a day when all the Palestinians would be able to return to their motherland.

EARLY POLITICAL INTEREST

At seventeen, Arafat was already contributing to the Palestine national cause. He smuggled weapons from Egypt to Palestine ahead of the 1948 war. He started wearing the *keffiyeh*, the traditional head dress of the Palestinians, and continued wearing it for the rest of his life; ultimately, it has become a symbol of his nationality.

Arafat and his associates founded the organization Al-Fatah, the main objective of which was to form armed resistance against Israel and win back the land that had been taken over by Israel in 1948.

FORMATION OF PLO

The founding of the Palestine Liberation Organization (PLO) was an important move in the history of Palestine as it brought together everyone towards a free Palestine. A war broke out between Arab and Israel in 1967. Israel won but Yasser Arafat became a popular leader. His organization, Al-Fatah was the only fighting force left and it started taking a key role in the Palestinian movements. He became the chairman of the executive committee of PLO in 1969.

In the years that followed, there were numerous cases of bombings and hijackings. In fact, the group was considered to be a terrorist organization by the US. He was forced to move to Lebanon after King Hussein of Jordan expelled him. By then, Arafat had realized that he had to seek a political solution instead of a military one as violent attempts had proven futile.

GUERRILLA TO STATESMAN

Yasser Arafat's status increased significantly and he came to be known worldwide. He became less of a guerrilla fighter and more of a statesman. Things changed when the UN in 1974 recognized the PLO as the 'sole representative of the Palestinian people'. In his famous speech, he said, 'I have come bearing an olive branch and a freedom fighter's gun. Do not let the olive branch fall from my hand.'

Arafat became the first representative of a non-governmental entity to address the UN general assembly. He got an international platform to talk about the grievances of his people. The year 1988 was a landmark in the history of Palestine as Arafat convinced the rest of the PLO workers to fight for Palestine statehood with Jerusalem as its capital along with Israel by its side.

Arafat had to agree to UN Security Council's Resolution 242 which directed to co-exist in peace and security, and denounce terrorism in all forms. Although this declaration opened many doors for Palestine, including that of the US, it also earned him enemies within Palestine as they thought that Arafat had betrayed their cause. He signed a peace treaty with the prime minister of Israel.

DEATH

In 1996, Arafat was elected as the president of the newly-elected Palestinian Authority. But, by 2000, peace seemed to be at bay. He said that he was not ready to give up Jerusalem. Unfortunately, in 2004, Arafat fell ill and breathed his last.

DID YOU KNOW?

- Yasser Arafat has also been known as Mr Palestine which might have started as a joke but it stuck to him.
- Arafat shared the Nobel Peace Prize along with Israel's Shimon Peres and Yitzhak Rabin in 1994.
- It is suspected that Arafat's death was not natural and he was poisoned.

ZAKIR HUSAIN

Dr Zakir Husain, the third president of India, was a great visionary and statesman who understood the importance of education in moulding a nation. Dr Husain spent his life trying to build a bridge between politics and education.

EARLY LIFE

Dr Zakir Husain was born on 8 February 1897 in Hyderabad to Fida Husain Khan and Naznin Begum. His ancestors came and settled in Qaimganj, Uttar Pradesh from Afganisthan. Unfortunately, he lost his father at a young age of ten after which his mother moved back to Qaimganj with all her children.

Husain received his early education in Parsi and Urdu at his home. He was very attached to his mother and didn't want to part from her, even for receiving education. Thus, she had to coax him to go to Etawah and receive schooling from Islamia High School. He was a good debater at school and his academic performance was praiseworthy. However, tragedy again struck the young Zakir when he lost his mother too at fourteen. Husain continued with his studies with vigour so as to fulfil his mother's dream.

ENTRY INTO POLITICS

Zakir Husain exhibited the qualities of a leader in college and went on to become a prominent student leader. He was influenced by the ideas of Moulana Azad and Mohammed Ali, and the feelings of nationalism were deeply sown in his mind.

When Gandhiji gave a clarion call to the nation to be a part of the non-cooperation movement, young Zakir, who was in college at that time, was so influenced that he decided to actively participate in the movement. The principal of his college offered him a lucrative job if he didn't participate in the movement but, Zakir refused the offer and joined the movement.

EDUCATIONIST

After leaving college and refusing to pursue education under the British rule, he was struck by the idea of opening a university which would be run by the Indians and would also have Indian teachers. In 1920, Zakir Husain, along with a few students and teachers, founded the National Muslim University (Jamia Millia) at Aligarh. He worked as a teacher for two years in Jamia Millia and tried to lay a strong foundation of the university.

In 1922, Zakir Husain left for Germany to receive a doctorate degree. On his return after three years, he was saddened to find Jamia Millia in a poor state. He again made efforts to reclaim its previous glory and, on the advice of Gandhiji, shifted the university from Aligarh to Delhi.

At the age of twenty-nine, Husain became the principal of the university and followed the ideology of Mahatma Gandhi. He provided free education to students from villages till class VII. Along with academics, the children were also given vocational education. Husain supported a work-centered education rather than a book-centered one and gave a lot of importance to value education. Influenced by the ideology of simple living and high thinking, Husain lived his life on the ideals of Gandhiji.

PRESIDENT OF INDIA

Dr Zakir Husain continued as the vice chancellor of Jamia Millia till 1956, when he was nominated as a member of the Rajya Sabha. He was appointed the governor of Bihar from 1957 to 1962. In 1962, he was appointed as the vice president where he served his term for five years. On 13 May 1967, he was elected as the president of India.

DEATH AND LEGACY

Dr Husain has been the only president who breathed his last, on 3 May 1969, while still in office. He was known for his great sense of humanity. He was also awarded the Padma Bhushan and the Bharat Ratna.

DID YOU KNOW?

- His father was a lawyer and Zakir was the third of seven children.
- He was responsible for the launch of Basic National Education in 1938.
- He was awarded the DLitt by the universities of Delhi, Calcutta, Aligarh, Allahabad and Cairo.

CONCLUSION

The journey to great leadership is mired with countless struggles and possibilities. This book is an attempt to dwell on the world of leadership to identify and analyse qualities that made a great leader. No wonder the journey was full of new discoveries and amazement at every step. These people have brought in such difference to the world that one is forced to wonder how this world would have shaped-up without these legendary men and women.

The courage of Golda Meir, patriotism of Subhas Chandra Bose or the infectious zeal of Che Guevera surely leaves behind strong lessons that can inspire youngsters to become agents of change in their respective communities. Mustafa Kemal Ataturk made laudable efforts to give an identity to Turkey while Mandela sought to earn dignity and liberty for his fellow beings. Children can emulate these legends and try to bring forth a positive change in their lives and the lives of all others around them.

In this book, I have made a conscious effort to keep all the microcosmic details on these towering global personalities intact. I am sure that children will immensely benefit from this tour across the life and achievements of these remarkable men and women. This book will kindle young minds and enable them to develop a keen desire to learn about these noteworthy pathfinders from across the world and imbibe particular traits from them, which would eventually help shape the future leaders of the world.

My association with the book has been momentous and it has helped me broaden my horizon and deepen my understanding of the world. I am sure it will do the same to all our young readers.

ACKNOWLEDGEMENTS

This book could see the light of the day because of the support I received from several quarters. First, I remain grateful to my parents, N.K. Biswas and Uma Biswas for their consistent belief in me. My mother has always been an inspiration and a pillar of strength for me. I also owe a lot to my daughter, Pakhi, for inspiring me through her own little ways.

The research in this book would have been incomplete without the support of my husband, Alan Clifton. Thank you for your wise suggestions and advice when I needed it the most. I also appreciate the moral support lent to me by my younger sister, Suparna.

Finally, I am immensely grateful to the brilliant editorial team of Rupa Publications for guiding me throughout the evolution of this book.